"That comes naturally to you, doesn't it?"

"Rescuing damsels in distre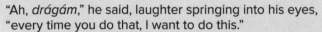

"No, that slow, sexy, let's-ge

"Is that the message it send

"Yes."

"Is it working?"

She pursed her lips. "No."

"Ah, *drágám*," he said, laughter springing into his eyes, "every time you do that, I want to do this."

She'd thought it would end there. One touch. One pass of his mouth over hers. It *should* have ended there. Traffic was coursing along the busy street, for pity's sake. A streetcar clanged by. Yet Natalie didn't move as his arm went around her waist, drawing her closer, while her pulse pounded in her veins.

She was breathing hard when Dominic lifted his head. So was he, she saw with intense relief. She couldn't remember if she'd ever kissed a man on a public sidewalk in the middle of the afternoon before. She didn't think so. Somehow it didn't seem like something she would do. If she had, though, she hoped it hit him with the same impact it had her.

* * *

Her Unforgettable Royal Lover
is part of The Duchess Diaries series: Two royal granddaughters on their way to happily-ever-after!

* * *

If you're on Twitter,
tell us what you think of Harlequin Desire!
#harlequindesire

Dear Reader,

As a history buff, I've read extensively about the Austrian-Hungarian Empire. Also about one of that empire's most tragic figures—Elisabeth Amalie Eugenie, Empress of Austria and Queen of Hungary. Sisi, as she was known, lost her only son in a tragic murder-suicide pact. She herself was assassinated by an anarchist in Geneva, Switzerland, in 1898.

Recently, my husband and I seemed to be tracing Sisi's footsteps in our travels. We visited the Hapsburg Palaces in Vienna and Budapest, her retreat in Corfu and many hunting lodges and grand hotels where she stayed. And the more I learned about this incredibly beautiful, charismatic woman, the more I wanted to craft a modern-day character along her royal lines.

Thus the Duchess Diaries—and Charlotte, the grand duchess of Karlenburgh—were born. I hope you've enjoyed Charlotte and the St. Sebastians as much as I have. Now settle back and prepare for fireworks as beautiful, brainy Dr. Zia St. Sebastian tangles with a very determined Texan.

Merline Lovelace

HER UNFORGETTABLE ROYAL LOVER

—

MERLINE LOVELACE

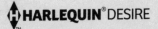

Recycling programs
for this product may
not exist in your area.

ISBN-13: 978-0-373-73359-0

Her Unforgettable Royal Lover

Copyright © 2014 by Merline Lovelace

Printed in U.S.A.

Books by Merline Lovelace

Harlequin Desire

The Paternity Proposition #2145
The Paternity Promise #2163
Ω*A Business Engagement* #2256
Ω*The Diplomat's Pregnant Bride* #2274
Ω*Her Unforgettable Royal Lover* #2346

Silhouette Desire

*Devlin and the Deep Blue Sea #1726
Δ*The CEO's Christmas Proposition* #1905
Δ*The Duke's New Year's Resolution* #1913
Δ*The Executive's Valentine Seduction* #1917

Harlequin Romantic Suspense

*Strangers When We Meet #1660
*Double Deception #1667

Silhouette Romantic Suspense

*Diamonds Can Be Deadly #1411
*Closer Encounters #1439
*Stranded with a Spy #1483

*Match Play #1500
*Undercover Wife #1531
**Seduced by the
   Operative* #1589
*Risky Engagement #1613
**Danger in the
   Desert* #1640

Harlequin Nocturne

Mind Games #37
***Time Raiders:
   The Protector* #75

*Code Name: Danger
ΔHolidays Abroad
**Time Raiders
ΩDuchess Diaries

Other titles by this author
available in ebook format.

MERLINE LOVELACE

A career Air Force officer, Merline Lovelace served at bases all over the world. When she hung up her uniform for the last time she decided to combine her love of adventure with a flair for storytelling, basing many of her tales on her own experiences in uniform. Since then she's produced more than ninety action-packed sizzlers, many of which have made the *USA TODAY* and Waldenbooks bestseller lists. Over eleven million copies of her books are available in some thirty countries.

When she's not tied to her keyboard, Merline enjoys reading, chasing little white balls around the fairways of Oklahoma and traveling to new and exotic locales with her handsome husband, Al. Check her website at www.merlinelovelace.com or friend her on Facebook for news and information about her latest releases.

To Neta and Dave, friends, traveling buds and the source of all kinds of fodder for my books. Thanks for the info on research grants and nasty bugs, Neta!

Prologue

Who would have imagined my days would become this rich and full, and at such a late point in my life! My darling granddaughter Sarah and her husband, Dev, have skillfully blended marriage with their various enterprises, their charitable work and their travels to all parts of the world. Yet Sarah still finds time to involve me in the book she's writing on lost treasures of the art world. My input has been limited, to be sure, but I've very much enjoyed being part of such an ambitious undertaking.

And Eugenia, my carefree, high-spirited Eugenia, has surprised herself by becoming the most amazing wife and mother. Her twins are very much like she was at that age. Bright-eyed and lively, with very distinct personalities. And best of all, her husband, Jack, is being considered for appointment as US Ambassador to the United Nations. If he's confirmed, he and Gina and the babies would live only a few blocks away.

Until that happens, I have the company of my longtime friend and companion, Maria. And Anastazia, my lovely, so serious Anastazia. Zia's in her second year of a residency in pediatric medicine and I played shamelessly on our somewhat tenuous kinship to convince her to live with me for the three-year program. She wears herself to the bone, poor dear, but Maria and I see that she eats well and gets at least some rest.

It's her brother, Dominic, I fret about. Dom insists he's not ready to settle down, and why should he with all the women who throw themselves at him? His job worries me, however. It's too dangerous, too high-risk. I do wish he would quit working undercover, and may have found just the enticement to encourage him to do so. How surprised he'll be when I tell him about the document Sarah's clever research assistant has discovered!

From the diary of Charlotte,
Grand Duchess of Karlenburgh

One

August was slamming New York City when Dominic St. Sebastian climbed out of a cab outside the castle-like Dakota. Heat waves danced like demented demons above the sidewalks. Across the street, moisture-starved leaves drifted like yellowed confetti from the trees in Central Park. Even the usual snarl of cabs and limos and sightseeing buses cruising the Upper West Side seemed lethargic and sluggish.

The same couldn't be said for the Dakota's doorman. As dignified as ever in his lightweight summer uniform, Jerome abandoned his desk to hold the door for the new arrival.

"Thanks," Dom said with the faint accent that marked him as European despite the fact that English came as naturally to him as his native Hungarian. Shifting his carryall to his right hand, he clapped the older man's shoulder with his left. "How's the duchess?"

"As strong-willed as ever. She wouldn't listen to the rest of us, but Zia finally convinced her to forego her daily constitutional during this blistering heat."

Dom wasn't surprised his sister had succeeded where others failed. Anastazia Amalia Julianna St. Sebastian combined the slashing cheekbones, exotic eyes and stunning beauty of a supermodel with the tenacity of a bulldog.

And now his beautiful, tenacious sister was living with

Grand Duchess Charlotte. Zia and Dom had met their long-lost relative for the first time only last year and formed an instant bond. So close a bond that Charlotte had invited Zia to live at the Dakota during her pediatric residency at Mt. Sinai.

"Has my sister started her new rotation?" Dom asked while he and Jerome waited for the elevator.

He didn't doubt the doorman would know. He had the inside track on most of the Dakota's residents but kept a close eye on his list of favorites. Topping that list were Charlotte St. Sebastian and her two granddaughters, Sarah and Gina. Zia had recently been added to the select roster.

"She started last week," Jerome advised. "She doesn't say so, but I can see oncology is hard on her. Would be on anyone, diagnosing and treating all those sick children. And the hospital works the residents to the bone, which doesn't help." He shook his head, but brightened a moment later. "Zia wrangled this afternoon off, though, when she heard you were flying in. Oh, and Lady Eugenia is here, too. She arrived last night with the twins."

"I haven't seen Gina and the twins since the duchess's birthday celebration. The girls must be, what? Six or seven months old now?"

"Eight." Jerome's seamed face folded into a grin. Like everyone else, he'd fallen hard for an identical pair of rose-bud mouths, lake-blue eyes and heads topped with their mother's spun-sugar, silvery-blond curls.

"Lady Eugenia says they're crawling now," he warned. "Better watch where you step and what you step in."

"I will," Dom promised with a grin.

As the elevator whisked him to the fifth floor, he remembered the twins as he'd last seen them. Cooing and blowing bubbles and waving dimpled fists, they'd already developed into world-class heartbreakers.

They'd since developed two powerful sets of lungs,

Dom discovered when a flushed and flustered stranger yanked open the door.

"It's about time! We've been..."

She stopped, blinking owlishly behind her glasses, while a chorus of wails rolled down the marble-tiled foyer.

"You're not from Osterman's," she said accusingly.

"The deli? No, I'm not."

"Then who...? Oh! You're Zia's brother." Her nostrils quivered, as if she'd suddenly caught a whiff of something unpleasant. "The one who goes through women like a hot knife through butter."

Dom hooked a brow but couldn't dispute the charge. He enjoyed the company of women. Particularly the generously curved, pouty-lipped, out-for-a-good-time variety.

The one facing him now certainly didn't fall into the first two of those categories. Not that he could see more than a suggestion of a figure inside her shapeless linen dress and boxy jacket. Her lips were anything but pouty, however. Pretty much straight-lined, as a matter of fact, with barely disguised disapproval.

"Igen," Dom agreed lazily in his native Hungarian. "I'm Dominic. And you are?"

"Natalie," she bit out, wincing as the howls behind her rose to high-pitched shrieks. "Natalie Clark. Come in, come in."

Dom had spent almost seven years now as an Interpol agent. During that time, he'd helped take down his share of drug traffickers, black marketeers and the scum who sold young girls and boys to the highest bidders. Just last year he'd helped foil a kidnapping and murder plot against Gina's husband right here in New York City. But the scene that greeted him as he paused at the entrance to the duchess's elegant sitting room almost made him turn tail and run.

A frazzled Gina was struggling to hang on to a red-faced, furiously squirming infant in a frilly dress and a lacy headband with a big pink bow. Zia had her arms full with the second, equally enraged and similarly attired baby. The duchess sat straight-backed and scowling in regal disapproval, while the comfortably endowed Honduran who served as her housekeeper and companion stood at the entrance to the kitchen, her face screwed into a grimace as the twins howled their displeasure.

Thankfully, the duchess reached her limit before Dom was forced to beat a hasty retreat. Her eyes snapping, she gripped the ivory handle of her cane in a blue-veined, white-knuckled fist.

"Charlotte!" The cane thumped the floor. Once. Twice. "Amalia! You will kindly cease that noise at once."

Dom didn't know whether it was the loud banging or the imperious command that did the trick, but the howls cut off like a faucet and surprise leaped into four tear-drenched eyes. Blessed silence reigned except for the babies' gulping hiccups.

"Thank you," the duchess said coolly. "Gina, why don't you and Zia take the girls to the nursery? Maria will bring their bottles as soon as Osterman's delivers the milk."

"It should be here any moment, *Duquesa*." Using her ample hips, the housekeeper backed through the swinging door to the kitchen. "I'll get the bottles ready."

Gina was headed for the hall leading to the bedrooms when she spotted her cousin four or five times removed. "Dom!" She blew him an air kiss. "I'll talk to you when I get the girls down."

"I, as well," his sister said with a smile in her dark eyes.

He set down his carryall and crossed the elegant sitting room to kiss the duchess's cheeks. Her paper-thin skin carried the faint scent of gardenias, and her eyes were cloudy with age but missed little. Including the wince he couldn't quite hide when he straightened.

"Zia told me you'd been knifed. Again."

"Just nicked a rib."

"Yes, well, we need to talk about these nicked ribs and bullet wounds you collect with distressing frequency. But first, pour us a…" She broke off at the buzz of the doorbell. "That must be the delivery. Natalie, dear, would you sign for it and take the milk to Maria?"

"Of course."

Dom watched the stranger head back to the foyer and turned to the duchess. "Who is she?"

"A research assistant Sarah hired to help with her book. Her name's Natalie Clark and she's part of what I want to talk to you about."

Dominic knew Sarah, the duchess's older granddaughter, had quit her job as an editor at a glossy fashion magazine when she married self-made billionaire Devon Hunter. He also knew Sarah had expanded on her degree in art history from the Sorbonne by hitting every museum within taxi distance when she accompanied Dev on his business trips around the world. That—and the fact that hundreds of years of art had been stripped off walls and pedestals when the Soviets overran the Duchy of Karlenburgh decades ago—had spurred Sarah to begin documenting what she learned about the lost treasures of the art world. It also prompted a major New York publisher to offer a fat, six-figure advance if she turned her notes into a book.

What Dom *didn't* know was what Sarah's book had to do with him, much less the female now making her way to the kitchen with an Osterman's delivery sack in hand. Sarah's research assistant couldn't be more than twenty-five or twenty-six but she dressed like a defrocked nun. Mousy-brown hair clipped at her neck. No makeup. Square glasses with thick lenses. Sensible flats and that shapeless linen dress.

When the kitchen door swung behind her, Dom had to

ask. "How is this Natalie Clark involved in what you want to talk to me about?"

The duchess waived an airy hand. "Pour us a *pálinka*, and I'll tell you."

"Should you have brandy? Zia said in her last email that…"

"Pah! Your sister fusses more than Sarah and Gina combined."

"With good reason, yes? She's a doctor. She has a better understanding of your health issues."

"Dominic." The duchess leveled a steely stare. "I've told my granddaughters, I've told your sister, and I'll tell you. The day I can't handle an aperitif before dinner is the day you may bundle me off to a nursing home."

"The day you can't drink us all under the table, you mean." Grinning, Dom went to the sideboard and lined up two cut-crystal snifters.

Ah, but he was a handsome devil, Charlotte thought with a sigh. Those dark, dangerous eyes. The slashing brows and glossy black hair. The lean, rangy body inherited from the wiry horsemen who'd swept down from the Steppes on their sturdy ponies and ravaged Europe. Magyar blood ran in his veins, as it did in hers, combined with but not erased by centuries of intermarriage among the royals of the once-great Austro-Hungarian Empire.

The Duchy of Karlenburgh had been part of that empire. A tiny part, to be sure, but one with a history that had stretched back for seven hundred years. It now existed only in dusty history books, and one of those books was about to change Dominic's life. Hopefully for the better, although Charlotte doubted he would think so. Not at first. But with time…

She glanced up as the instigator of that change returned to the sitting room. "Ah, here you are, Natalie. We're just about to have an aperitif. Will you join us?"

"No, thank you."

Dom paused with his hand on the stopper of the Bohemian crystal decanter he and Zia had brought the duchess as a gift for their first meeting. Thinking to soften the researcher's stiff edges, he gave her a slow smile.

"Are you sure? This apricot brandy is a specialty of my country."

"I'm sure."

Dom blinked. *Mi a fene!* Did her nose just quiver again? As though she'd picked up another bad odor? What the hell kind of tales had Zia and/or Gina fed the woman?

Shrugging, he splashed brandy into two snifters and carried one to the duchess. But if anyone could use a shot of *pálinka*, he thought as he folded his long frame into the chair beside his great-aunt's, the research assistant could. The double-distilled, explosively potent brandy would set more than her nostrils to quivering.

"How long will you be in New York?" the duchess asked after downing a healthy swallow.

"Only tonight. I have a meeting in Washington tomorrow."

"Hmm. I should wait until Zia and Gina return to discuss this with you, but they already know about it."

"About what?"

"The Edict of 1867." She set her brandy aside, excitement kindling in her faded blue eyes. "As you may remember from your history books, war with Prussia forced Emperor Franz Joseph to cede certain concessions to his often rambunctious Hungarian subjects. The Edict of 1867 gave Hungary full internal autonomy as long as it remained part of the empire for purposes of war and foreign affairs."

"Yes, I know this."

"Did you also know Karlenburgh added its own codicil to the agreement?"

"No, I didn't, but then I would have no reason to," Dom

said gently. "Karlenburgh is more your heritage than mine, Duchess. My grandfather—your husband's cousin—left Karlenburgh Castle long before I was born."

And the duchy had ceased to exist soon after that. World War I had carved up the once-mighty Austro-Hungarian Empire. World War II, the brutal repression of the Cold War era, the abrupt dissolution of the Soviet Union and vicious attempts at "ethnic cleansing" had all added their share of upheavals to the violently changing political landscape of Eastern Europe.

"Your grandfather took his name and his bloodline with him when he left Karlenburgh, Dominic." Charlotte leaned closer and gripped his arm with fingers that dug in like talons. "You inherited that bloodline and that name. You're a St. Sebastian. And the present Grand Duke of Karlenburgh."

"What?"

"Natalie found it during her research. The codicil. Emperor Franz Joseph reconfirmed that the St. Sebastians would carry the titles of Grand Duke and Duchess forever and in perpetuity in exchange for holding the borders of the empire. The empire doesn't exist anymore, but despite all the wars and upheavals, that small stretch of border between Austria and Hungary remains intact. So, therefore, does the title."

"On paper, perhaps. But the lands and outlying manors and hunting lodges and farmlands that once comprised the duchy have long since been dispersed and redeeded. It would take a fortune and decades in court to reclaim any of them."

"The lands and manor houses are gone, yes. Not the title. Sarah will become Grand Duchess when I die. Or Gina if, God forbid, something should happen to her sister. But they married commoners. According to the laws of primogeniture, their husbands can't assume the title of

Grand Duke. Until either Sarah or Gina has a son, or their daughters grow up and marry royalty, the only one who can claim it is you, Dom."

Right, he wanted to drawl. That and ten dollars would get him a half-decent espresso at one of New York's overpriced coffee bars.

He swallowed the sarcasm but lobbed a quick glare at the woman wearing an expression of polite interest, as if she hadn't initiated this ridiculous conversation with her research. He'd have a thing or two to say to Ms. Clark later about getting the duchess all stirred up over an issue that was understandably close to her heart but held little relevance to the real world. Particularly the world of an undercover operative.

He allowed none of those thoughts to show in his face as he folded Charlotte's hand between his. "I appreciate the honor you want to bestow on me, Duchess. I do. But in my line of work, I can hardly hang a title around my neck."

"Yes, I want to speak to you about that, too. You've been living on the edge for too many years now. How long can you continue before someone nicks more than a rib?"

"Exactly what I've been asking him," Zia commented as she swept into the sitting room with her long-legged stride.

She'd taken advantage of her few hours away from the hospital to pull on her favorite jeans and a summer tank top in blistering red. The rich color formed a striking contrast to her dark eyes and shoulder-length hair as black and glossy as her brother's. When he stood and opened his arms, she walked into them and hugged him with the same fierce affection he did her.

She was only four years younger than Dom, twenty-seven to his thirty-one, but he'd assumed full responsibility for his teenage sibling when their parents died. He'd been there, too, standing round-the-clock watch beside her hospital bed when she'd almost bled to death after a uterine cyst ruptured her first year at university. The complications that resulted from the rupture had changed her life in so many ways.

What hadn't changed was Dom's bone-deep protectiveness. No matter where his job took him or what dangerous enterprise he was engaged in, Zia had only to send a coded text and he would contact her within hours, if not minutes. Although he always shrugged off the grimmer aspects of his work, she'd wormed enough detail out of him over the years to add her urging to that of the duchess.

"You don't have to stay undercover. Your boss at Interpol told me he has a section chief job waiting for you whenever you want it."

"You can see me behind a desk, Zia-mia?"

"Yes!"

"What a poor liar you are." He made a fist and delivered a mock punch to her chin. "You wouldn't last five minutes under interrogation."

Gina had returned during their brief exchange. Shoving back her careless tumble of curls, she entered the fray. "Jack says you would make an excellent liaison to the State Department. In fact, he wants to talk to you about that tomorrow, when you're in Washington."

"With all due respect to your husband, Lady Eugenia, I'm not ready to join the ranks of bureaucrats."

His use of her honorific brought out one of Gina's merry, irreverent grins. "Since we're tossing around titles here, has Grandmother told you about the codicil?"

"She has."

"Well then…" Fanning out the skirts of her leafy-green sundress, she sank to the floor in an elegant, if theatrical, curtsy.

Dom muttered something distinctly unroyal under his breath. Fortunately, the Clark woman covered it when she pushed to her feet.

"Excuse me. This is a family matter. I'll leave you to discuss it and go back to my research. You'll call me when it's convenient for us to continue our interview, Duchess?"

"I will. You're in New York until Thursday, is that correct?"

"Yes, ma'am. Then I fly to Paris to compare notes with Sarah."

"We'll get together again before then."

"Thank you." She bent to gather the bulging briefcase that had been resting against the leg of her chair. Straightening, she nudged up her glasses back into place. "It was good to meet you, Dr. St. Sebastian, and to see you again, Lady Eugenia."

Her tone didn't change. Neither did her polite expression. But Dom didn't miss what looked very much like a flicker of disdain in her brown eyes when she dipped her head in his direction.

"Your Grace."

He didn't alter his expression, either, but both his sister and his cousin recognized the sudden, silky note in his voice.

"I'll see you to the door."

"Thank you, but I'll let myself… Oh. Uh, all right."

Natalie blinked owlishly behind her glasses. The smile didn't leave Dominic St. Sebastian's ridiculously handsome face and the hand banding her upper arm certainly wouldn't leave any bruises. That didn't make her feel any less like a suspect being escorted from the scene of a crime, however. Especially when he paused with a hand on the door latch and skewered her with a narrow glance from those dark eyes.

"Where are you staying?"

"I beg your pardon?"

"Where are you staying?"

Good Lord! Was he hitting on her? No, he couldn't

be! She was most definitely not his type. According to Zia's laughing reports, her bachelor brother went for leggy blondes or voluptuous brunettes. A long string of them, judging by the duchess's somewhat more acerbic references to his sowing altogether too many wild oats.

That more than anything had predisposed Natalie to dislike Dominic St. Sebastian sight unseen. She'd fallen for a too-handsome, too-smooth operator like him once and would pay for that stupidity for the rest of her life. Still, she tried, she really tried, to keep disdain from seeping into her voice as she tugged her arm free.

"I don't believe where I'm staying is any of your business."

"You've made it my business with this nonsense about a codicil."

Whoa! He could lock a hand around her arm. He could perp-walk her to the door. He could *not* disparage her research.

Thoroughly indignant, Natalie returned fire. "It's not nonsense, as you would know if you'd displayed any interest in your family's history. I suggest you show a little more respect for your heritage, *Your Grace*, and for the duchess."

He muttered something in Hungarian she suspected was not particularly complimentary and bent an elbow against the doorjamb, leaning close. Too close! She could see herself in his pupils, catch the tang of apricot brandy on his breath.

"My respect for Charlotte is why you and I are going to have a private chat, yes? I ask again, where are you staying?"

His Magyar roots were showing, Natalie noted with a skitter of nerves. The slight thickening of his accent should have warned her. Should have sent her scurrying back into the protective shell she'd lived inside for so long it was now as much a part of her life as her drab hair and clothes. But some spark of her old self tilted her chin.

"You're supposed to be a big, bad secret agent," she said coolly. "Dig out the information yourself."

He would, Dom vowed as the door closed behind her with a small thud. He most definitely would.

Two

All it took was one call to arm Dom with the essential information. Natalie Elizabeth Clark. Born Farmington, Illinois. Age twenty-nine, height five feet six inches, brown hair, brown eyes. Single. Graduated University of Michigan with a degree in library science, specializing in archives and presentation. Employed as an archivist with Centerville Community College for three years, the State of Illinois Civil Service Board for four. Currently residing in L.A. where she was employed by Sarah St. Sebastian as a personal assistant.

An archivist. Christ!

Dom shook his head as his cab picked its way downtown later that evening. He envisioned a small cubicle, her head bent toward a monitor screen, her eyes staring through those thick lenses at an endless stream of documents to be verified, coded and electronically filed. And she'd done it for seven years! Dom would have committed ritual hara-kiri after a week. No wonder she'd jumped when Sarah put out feelers for an assistant to help research her book.

Ms. Clark was still running endless computer searches. Still digging through archives, some electronic, some paper. But at least now she was traveling the globe to get at the most elusive of those documents. And, Dom guessed as his cab pulled up at the W New York, doing that traveling on a very generous expense account.

He didn't bother to stop at the front desk. His phone call had confirmed that Ms. Clark had checked into room 1304 two days ago. And a tracking program developed for the military and now in use by a number of intelligence agencies confirmed her cell phone was currently emitting signals from this location.

Two minutes later Dom rapped on her door. The darkening of the peephole told him she was as careful in her personal life as she no doubt was in her work. He smiled his approval, then waited for the door to open.

When neither of those events happened, he rapped again. Still no response.

"It's Dominic St. Sebastian, Ms. Clark. I know you're in there. You may as well open the door."

She complied but wasn't happy about it. "It's generally considered polite to call ahead for an appointment instead of just showing up at someone's hotel room."

The August humidity had turned her shapeless linen dress into a roadmap of wrinkles, and her sensible pumps had been traded for hotel flip-flops. She'd freed her hair from the clip, though, and it framed her face in surprisingly thick, soft waves as she tipped Dom a cool look through her glasses.

"May I ask why you felt compelled to come all the way downtown to speak with me?"

Dom had been asking himself the same thing. He'd confirmed this woman was who she said she was and verified her credentials. The truth was he probably wouldn't have given Natalie Clark a second thought if not for those little nose quivers.

He'd told himself the disdain she'd wiped off her face so quickly had triggered his cop's instinct. Most of the scum he'd dealt with over the years expressed varying degrees of contempt for the police, right up until they were cuffed and led away. His sister, however, would probably insist those small hints of derision had pricked his male ego. It was true that Dom could never resist a challenge. But despite Zia's frequent assertions to the contrary, he didn't try to finesse *every* female who snagged his attention into bed.

Still, he was here and here he intended to remain until he satisfied his curiosity about this particular female. "I'd like more information on this codicil you've uncovered, Ms. Clark."

"I'm sure you would. I'll be happy to email you the documentation I've…"

"I prefer to see what you have now. May I come in, or do we continue our discussion in the hall?"

Her mouth pursing, she stood aside. Her obvious reluctance intrigued Dom. And, all right, stirred his hunting instincts. Too bad he had that meeting at the National Central Bureau—the US branch of Interpol—in Washington tomorrow. It might have been interesting to see what it would take to get those prim, disapproving lips to unpurse and sigh his name.

He skimmed a glance around the room. Two queen beds, one with her open briefcase and neat stacks of files on it. An easy chair angled to get the full benefit of the high-definition flat-screen. A desk with a black ergonomic chair, another stack of files and a seventeen-inch laptop open to a webpage displaying a close-up of an elaborately jeweled egg.

"One of the Fabergé eggs?" he asked, moving closer to admire the sketch of a gem-encrusted egg nested in a two-wheeled gold cart.

"Yes."

"The Cherub with a Chariot," Dom read, "a gift from Tsar Alexander III to his wife, Maria Fyodorovna for Easter, 1888. One of eight Fabergé eggs currently lost."

He glanced at the researcher hovering protectively close to her work, as if to protect it from prying eyes.

"And you're on the hunt for it?"

"I'm documenting its history."

Her hand crept toward the laptop's lid, as if itching to slam it down.

"What have you found so far?"

The lips went tight again, but Dom was too skilled at interrogations to let her off the hook. He merely waited until she gave a grudging nod.

"Documents show it was at Gatchina Palace in 1891, and was one of forty or so eggs sent to the armory at the Kremlin after the 1917 Revolution. Some experts believe it was purchased in the 1930s by Victor and Armand Hammer. But…"

He could see when her fascination with her work overcame her reluctance to discuss it. Excitement snuck into her voice and added a spark to her brown eyes. Her very velvety, very enticing brown eyes, he thought as she tugged off her glasses and twirled them by one stem.

"I found a reference to a similar egg sold at an antiques shop in Paris in 1930. A shop started by a Russian émigré. No one knows how the piece came into his possession, but I've found a source I want to check when I'm in Paris next week. It may…"

She caught herself and brought the commentary to an abrupt halt. The twirling ceased. The glasses whipped up, and wariness replaced the excitement in the doe-brown eyes.

"I'm not trying to pump you for information," Dom assured her. "Interpol has a whole division devoted to lost, stolen or looted cultural treasures, you know."

"Yes, I do."

"Since you're heading over to Paris, I can set up a meeting for you with the division chief, if you like."

The casual offer seemed to throw her off balance. "I… Uh… I have access to their database but…" Her glance went to the screen, then came back to Dom. "I would appreciate that," she said stiffly. "Thank you."

A grin sketched across his face. "There now. That didn't taste so bad going down, did it?"

Instant alarms went off in Natalie's head. She could almost hear their raucous clanging as she fought to keep her chin high and her expression politely remote. She would *not* let a lazy grin and a pair of glinting, bedroom eyes seduce her. Not again. Never again.

"I'll give you my business card," she said stiffly. "Your associate can reach me anytime at my mobile number or by email."

"So cool, so polite." He didn't look at the embossed card she retrieved from her briefcase, merely slipped it into the pocket of his slacks. "What is it about me you don't like?"

How about everything!

"I don't know you well enough to dislike you." She should have left it there. Would have, if he hadn't been standing so close. "Nor," she added with a shrug, "do I wish to."

She recognized her error at once. Men like Dominic St. Sebastian would take that as a challenge. Hiding a grimace, Natalie attempted some quick damage control.

"You said you wanted more information on the codicil. I have a scanned copy on my computer. I'll pull it up and print out a copy for you."

She pulled out the desk chair. He was forced to step back so she could sit, but any relief she might have gained from the small separation dissipated when he leaned a hand on the desk and bent to peer over her shoulder. His breath stirred the loose tendrils at her temple, moved lower, washed warm and hot against her ear. She managed to keep from hunching her shoulder but it took an iron effort of will.

"So that's it," he said as the scanned image appeared, "the document the duchess thinks makes me a duke?"

"Grand Duke," Natalie corrected. "Excuse me, I need to check the paper feed in the printer."

There was nothing wrong with the paper feed. Her little portable printer had been cheerfully spitting out copies before St. Sebastian so rudely interrupted her work. But it was the best excuse she could devise to get him to stop breathing down her neck!

He took the copy and made himself comfortable in the armchair while he tried to decipher the spidery script. Natalie was tempted to let him suffer through the embellished High German, but relented and printed out a translation.

"I stumbled across the codicil while researching the Canaletto that once hung in the castle at Karlenburgh," she told him. "I'd found an obscure reference to the painting in the Austrian State Archives in Vienna."

She couldn't resist an aside. So many uninformed thought her profession dry and dull. They couldn't imagine the thrill that came with following one fragile thread to another, then another, and another.

"The archives are so vast, it's taken years to digitize them all. But the results are amazing. Really amazing. The oldest document dates back to 816."

He nodded, not appearing particularly interested in this bit of trivia that Natalie found so fascinating. Deflated, she got back to the main point.

"The codicil was included in a massive collection of letters, charters, treaties and proclamations relating to the Austro-Prussian War. Basically, it states what the duchess told you earlier. Emperor Franz Joseph granted the St. Sebastians the honor of Karlenburgh in perpetuity in exchange for defending the borders for the empire. The duchy may not exist anymore and so many national lines have been redrawn. That section of the border between

Austria and Hungary has held steady, however, through all the wars and invasions. So, therefore, has the title."

He made a noise that sounded close to a snort. "You and I both know this document isn't worth the paper you've just printed it on."

Offended on behalf of archivists everywhere, she cocked her chin. "The duchess disagrees."

"Right, and that's what you and I need to talk about."

He stuffed the printout in his pocket and pinned her with a narrow stare. No lazy grin now. No laughter in those dark eyes.

"Charlotte St. Sebastian barely escaped Karlenburgh with her life. She carried her baby in her arms while she marched on foot for some twenty or thirty miles through winter snows. I know the story is that she managed to bring away a fortune in jewels, as well. I'm not confirming the story…"

He didn't have to. Natalie had already pieced it together from her own research and from the comments Sarah had let drop about the personal items the duchess had disposed of over the years to raise her granddaughters in the style she considered commensurate with their rank.

"…but I am warning you not to take advantage of the duchess's very natural desire to see her heritage continue."

"Take advantage?"

It took a moment for that to sink in. When it did, she could barely speak through the anger that spurted hot and sour into her throat.

"Do you think…? Do you think this codicil is part of some convoluted scheme on my part to extract money from the St. Sebastians?"

Furious, she shoved to her feet. He rose as well, as effortlessly as an athlete, and countered her anger with a shrug.

"Not at this point. If I discover differently, however, you and I will most certainly have another chat."

"Get out!"

Maybe after she cooled down Natalie would admit flinging out an arm and stabbing a finger toward the door was overly melodramatic. At the moment, though, she wanted to slam that door so hard it knocked this pompous ass on his butt. Especially when he lifted a sardonic brow.

"Shouldn't that be 'Get out, *Your Grace*'?"

Her back teeth ground together. "Get. Out."

As a cab hauled him back uptown for a last visit with the duchess and his sister, Dom couldn't say his session with Ms. Clark had satisfied his doubts. There was still something he couldn't pin down about the researcher. She dressed like a bag lady in training and seemed content to efface herself in company. Yet when she'd flared up at him, when fury had brought color surging to her cheeks and fire to her eyes, the woman was anything but ignorable.

She reminded him of the mounts his ancestors had ridden when they'd swept down from the Steppes into the Lower Danube region. Their drab, brown-and-dun-colored ponies lacked the size and muscle power of destriers that carried European knights into battle. Yet the Magyars had wreaked havoc for more than half a century throughout Italy, France, Germany and Spain before finally being defeated by the Holy Roman Emperor Otto I.

And like one of those tough little ponies, Dom thought with a slow curl in his belly, Ms. Clark needed taming. She might hide behind those glasses and shapeless dresses, but she had a temper on her when roused. Too bad he didn't have time to gentle her to his hand. The exercise would be a hell of a lot more interesting than the meetings he had lined up in Washington tomorrow. Still, he entertained himself for the rest of the cab ride with various techniques he might employ should he cross paths with Natalie Elizabeth Clark anytime in the near future.

He'd pretty much decided he would make that happen when Zia let him into the duchess's apartment.

"Back so soon?" she said, her eyes dancing. "Ms. Clark didn't succumb to your manly charms and topple into bed with you?"

The quip was so close to Dom's recent thoughts that he answered more brusquely than he'd intended. *"I didn't go to her hotel to seduce her."*

"No? That must be a first."

"Jézus, Mária és József! The mouth on you, Anastazia Amalia. I should have washed it with soap when I had the chance."

"Ha! You would never have been able to hold me down long enough. But come in, come in! Sarah's on FaceTime with her grandmother. I think you'll be interested in their conversation."

FaceTime? The duchess? Marveling at the willingness of a woman who'd been born in the decades between two great world wars to embrace the latest in technology, Dom followed his sister into the sitting room. One glance at the tableau corrected his impression of Charlotte's geekiness.

She sat upright and unbending in her customary chair, her cane close at hand. An iPad was perched on her knees, but she was obviously not comfortable with the device. Gina sat cross-legged on the floor beside her, holding the screen to the proper angle

Sarah's voice floated through the speaker and her elegant features filled most of the screen. Her husband's filled the rest.

"I'm so sorry, Grandmama. It just slipped out."

"What slipped out?" Dom murmured to Zia.

"You," his sister returned with that mischievous glint in her eyes.

"Me?"

"Shh! Just listen."

Frowning, Dom tuned back into the conversation.

"Alexis called with an offer to hype my book in *Beguile*," Sarah was saying. "She wanted to play up both angles." Her nose wrinkled. "My former job at the magazine and my title. You know how she is."

"Yes," the duchess drawled. "I do."

"I told Alexis the book wasn't ready for hype yet. Unfortunately, I also told her we're getting there much quicker since I'd hired such a clever research assistant. I bragged about the letter Natalie unearthed in the House of Parma archives, the one from Marie Antoinette to her sister describing the miniature of her painted by Le Brun that went missing when the mob sacked Versailles. And..." She heaved a sigh. "I made the fatal mistake of mentioning the codicil Nat had stumbled across while researching the Canaletto."

Although the fact that Dom's cousin had mentioned that damned codicil set his internal antennae to vibrating, it didn't appear to upset the duchess. Mention of the Canaletto had brought a faraway look to her eyes.

"Your grandfather bought me that painting of the Grand Canal," she murmured to Sarah. "Right after I became pregnant with your mother."

She lapsed into a private reverie that neither of her granddaughters dared break. When she emerged a few moments later, she included them both in a sly smile.

"That's where it happened. In Venice. We were supposed to attend a *carnival* ball at Ari Onassis's palazzo. I'd bought the most gorgeous mask studded with pearls and lace. But...how does that rather obnoxious TV commercial go? You never know when the mood will hit you? All I can say is something certainly hit your grandfather that evening."

Gina hooted in delight. "Way to go, Grandmama!"

Sarah laughed, and her husband issued a joking curse. "Damn! My wife suggested we hit the carnival in Venice this spring but I talked her into an African photo safari instead."

"You'll know to listen to her next time," the duchess sniffed, although Dom would bet she knew the moment could strike as hot and heavy in the African savannah as it had in Venice.

"I don't understand," Gina put in from her perch on the floor. "What's the big deal about telling Alexis about the codicil?"

"Well…" Red crept into Sarah's cheeks. "I'm afraid I mentioned Dominic, too."

The subject of the conversation muttered a curse, and Gina let out another whoop. "Ooh, boy! Your barracuda of an editor is gonna latch on to that with both jaws. I foresee another top-ten edition, this one listing the sexiest single royals of the male persuasion."

"I know," her sister said miserably. "It'll be as bad as what Dev went through after he came out on *Beguile*'s top-ten list. When you see Dominic tell him I'm so, so sorry."

"He's right here." Hooking a hand, Gina motioned him over. "Tell him yourself."

When Dominic positioned himself in front of the iPad's camera, Sarah sent him a look of heartfelt apology. "I'm so sorry, Dom. I made Alexis promise she wouldn't go crazy with this, but…"

"But you'd better brace yourself, buddy," her husband put in from behind her shoulder. "Your life's about to get really, really complicated."

"I can handle it," Dom replied with more confidence than he was feeling at the moment.

"You think so, huh?" Dev returned with a snort. "Wait

till women start trying to stuff their phone number in your pants pocket and reporters shove mics and cameras in your face."

The first prospect hadn't sounded all that repulsive to Dom. The second he deemed highly unlikely...right up until he stepped out of a cab for his scheduled meeting at Washington's Interpol office the following afternoon and was blindsided by the pack of reporters, salivating at the scent of fresh blood.

"Your Highness! Over here!"

"Grand Duke!"

"Hey! Your lordship!"

Shaking his head at Americans' fixation on any and all things royal, he shielded his face with his hands like some damned criminal and pushed through the ravenous newshounds.

Three

Two weeks later Dominic was in a vicious mood. He had been since a dozen different American and European tabloids had splashed his face across their front pages, trumpeting the emergence of a long-lost Grand Duke.

When the stories hit, he'd expected the summons to Interpol Headquarters. He'd even anticipated his boss's suggestion that he take some of the unused vacation time he'd piled up over the years and lie low until the hoopla died down. He'd anticipated it, yes, but did *not* like being yanked off undercover duty and sent home to Budapest to twiddle his thumbs. And every time he thought the noise was finally dying down, his face popped up in another rag.

The firestorm of publicity had impacted his personal life, as well. Although Sarah's husband had tried to warn him, Dom had underestimated the reaction to his supposed royalty among the females of his acquaintance. The phone number he gave out to non-Interpol contacts had suddenly become very busy. Some of the callers were friends, some were former lovers. But many were strangers who'd wrangled the number out of *their* friends and weren't shy about wanting to get to know the new duke on a very personal level.

He'd turned most of them off with a laugh, a few of the more obnoxious with a curt suggestion they get a life. But one had sounded so funny and sexy over the phone that he'd arranged to meet her at a coffee bar. She turned out to be a tall, luscious brunette, as bright and engaging in person as she was over the phone. Dom was more than ready to agree with her suggestion they get a second cup to go and down it at her apartment or his loft. Before he could put in the order, though, she asked the waiter to take their picture with her cell phone. Damned if she hadn't zinged it off by email right there at the table. Just to a few friends, she explained with a smile. One, he discovered when yet another story hit the newsstands, just happened to be a reporter for a local tabloid.

In addition to the attention from strangers, the barrage of unwanted publicity seemed to make even his friends and associates view him through a different prism. To most of them he wasn't Dominic St. Sebastian anymore. He was Dominic, Grand Duke of a duchy that had ceased to exist a half century ago, for God's sake.

So he wasn't real happy when someone hammered on the door of his loft apartment on a cool September evening. Especially when the hammering spurred a chorus of ferocious barking from the hound who'd followed Dom home a year ago and decided to take up residence.

"Quiet!"

A useless command, since the dog considered announcing his presence to any and all visitors a sacred duty. Bred originally to chase down swiftly moving prey like deer and wolves, the Magyar Agár was as lean and fast as a greyhound. Dom had negotiated an agreement with his downstairs neighbors to dog-sit while he was on assignment, but man and beast had rebonded during this enforced vacation. Or at least the hound had. Dom had yet to reconcile himself to sharing his Gold Fassl with the pilsner-guzzling pooch.

"This better not be some damned reporter," he muttered as he kneed the still-barking hound aside and checked the spy hole. The special lens he'd had installed gave a

180-degree view of the landing outside his loft. The small area was occupied by two uniformed police officers and a bedraggled female Dom didn't recognize until he opened the door.

"Mi a fene!" he swore in Hungarian, then switched quickly to English. "Natalie! What happened to you?"

She didn't answer, being too preoccupied at the moment with the dog trying to shove his nose into her crotch. Dom swore again, got a grip on its collar and dislodged the nose, but he still didn't get a reply. She merely stared at him with a frown creasing her forehead and her hair straggling in limp tangles around her face.

"Are you Dominic St. Sebastian?" one of the police officers asked.

"Yes."

"Aka the Grand Duke?"

He made an impatient noise and kept his grip on the dog's collar. "Yes."

The second officer, whose nametag identified him as Gradjnic, glanced down at a newspaper folded to a grainy picture of Dom and the brunette at the coffee shop. "Looks like him," he volunteered.

His partner gestured to Natalie. "And you know this woman?"

"I do." Dom's glance raked the researcher, from her tangled hair to her torn jacket to what looked like a pair of men's sneakers several sizes too large for her. "What the devil happened to you?"

"Maybe we'd better come in," Gradjnic suggested.

"Yes, yes, of course."

The officers escorted Natalie inside, and Dom shut the dog in the bathroom before joining them. The Agár whined and scratched at the door but soon nosed out the giant chew-bones Dom stored in the hamper for emergencies like this.

Aside from the small bathroom, the loft consisted of a single, barn-like attic area that had once stored artifacts belonging to the Ethnological Museum. When the museum moved to new digs, their old building was converted to condos. Zia had just nailed a full scholarship to medical school, so Dom had decided to sink his savings into this loft apartment in the pricy Castle Hill district on the Buda side of the river. He'd then proceeded to sand and varnish the oak-plank floors to a high gloss. He'd also knocked out a section of the sloping roof and opened up a view of the Danube that usually had guests gasping.

Tonight's visitors were no exception. All three gawked at the floodlit spires, towering dome, flying buttresses and stained-glass windows of the Parliament Building across the river. Equally elaborate structures flanked the massive building, while the usual complement of river barges and brightly lit tour boats cruised by almost at its steps.

Ruthlessly, Dom cut into their viewing time. "Please sit down, all of you, then someone needs to tell me what this is all about."

"It's about this woman," Gradjnic said in heavily accented English when everyone had found a place to perch. He tugged a small black notebook from his shirt pocket. "What did you say her name was?"

Dom's glance shot to Natalie. "You didn't tell them your name?"

"I…I don't remember it."

"What?"

Her frown deepened. "I don't remember anything."

"Except the Grand Duke," Officer Gradjnic put in drily.

"Wait," Dom ordered. "Back up and start at the beginning."

Nodding, the policeman flipped through his notebook. "The beginning for us was 10:32 a.m. today, when dispatch called to report bystanders had fished a woman out of the

Danube. We responded, found this young lady sitting on the bank with her rescuers. She had no shoes, no purse, no cell phone, no ID of any kind and no memory of how she ended up in the river. When we asked her name or the name of a friend or relative here in Budapest, all she could tell us was 'the Grand Duke.'"

"Jesus!"

"She has a lump the size of a goose egg at the base of her skull, under her hair."

When Dom's gaze shot to Natalie again, she raised a tentative hand to the back of her neck. "More like a pigeon's egg," she corrected with a frown.

"Yes, well, the lump suggests she may have fallen off a bridge or a tour boat and hit her head on the way down, although none of the tour companies have reported a missing passenger. We had the EMTs take her to the hospital. The doctors found no sign of serious injury or concussion."

"No blurred vision?" Dom asked sharply. He'd taken—and delivered—enough blows to the head to know the warning signs. "No nausea or vomiting or balance problems?"

"Only the memory loss. The doctor said it's not all that unusual with that kind of trauma. Since we had no other place to take her, it was either leave her at the hospital or bring her to the only person she seems to know in Budapest—the Grand Duke."

Hit by a wicked sense of irony, Dom remembered those quivering nostrils and flickers of disdain. He suspected Ms. Clark would rather have been left at a dog pound than delivered to him.

"I'll take care of her," he promised, "but she must have a hotel room somewhere in the city."

"If she does, we'll let you know." Gradjnic flipped to an empty page and poised his pen. "Now what did you say her name was?"

"Natalie. Natalie Clark."

"American, we guessed from her accent."

"That's right."

"And she works for your cousin?"

"Yes, as research assistant." Angling around, Dom tried a tentative probe. "Natalie, you were supposed to meet with Sarah sometime this week. In Paris, right?"

"Sarah?"

"My cousin. Sarah St. Sebastian Hunter."

Her first response was a blank stare. Her second startled all three men.

"My head hurts." Scowling, she pushed out of her chair. "I'm tired. And these clothes stink."

With that terse announcement, she headed for the unmade bed at the far end of the loft. She kicked off the sneakers as she went. Dom lurched to his feet as she peeled out of the torn jacket.

"Hold on a minute!"

"I'm tired," she repeated. "I need sleep."

Shaking off his restraining hand, she flopped facedown across the bed. The three men watched with varying expressions of surprise and resignation as she buried her face in the pillow.

Gradjnic broke the small silence that followed. "Well, I guess that does it for us here. Now that we have her name, we'll trace Ms. Clark's entry into the country and her movements in Hungary as best we can. We'll also find out if she's registered at a hotel. And you'll call us when and if she remembers why she took that dive into the Danube, right?"

"Right."

The sound of their departure diverted the Agár's attention from the chew-bone he'd dug out of the hamper. To quiet his whining, Dom let him out of the bathroom but kept a close watch while he sniffed out the stranger sprawled sideways across the bed. Apparently deciding she posed no threat, the dog padded back to the living area and stretched out in front of the window to watch the brightly lit boats cruising up and down the river.

Dom had his phone in hand before the hound's speckled pink belly hit the planks. Five rings later, his sleepy-sounding cousin answered.

"Hullowhozzis?"

"It's Dom, Sarah."

"Dom?"

"Where are you?"

"We're in…uh…Dalian. China," she added, sounding more awake…and suddenly alarmed by a call in what had to be the middle of the night on the other side of the globe. "Is everyone okay? Grandmama? Gina? Zia? Oh, God! Is it one of the twins?"

"They're all fine, Sarah. But I can't say the same for your research assistant."

He heard a swift rustle of sheets. A headboard creaking.

"Dev! Wake up! Dom says something's happened to Natalie!"

"I'm awake."

"Tell me," Sarah demanded.

"The best guess is she fell off a bridge or a cruise boat. They fished her out of the river early this morning."

"Is she…? Is she dead?"

"No, but she's got a good-size lump at the base of her skull and she doesn't remember anything. Not even her name."

"Good Lord!" The sheets rustled again. "Natalie's been hurt, Dev. Would you contact your crew and have them prep the Gulfstream? I need to fly back to Paris right away."

"She's not in Paris," Dom interjected. "She's with me, in Budapest."

"In Budapest? But…how? Why?"

"I was hoping you could tell me."

"She didn't say anything about Hungary when we got together in Paris last week. Only that she might drive down to Vienna again, to do more research on the Canaletto." A note of accusation slipped through Sarah's concern. "She was also going to dig a little more on the codicil. Something you said about it seemed to have bothered her."

He'd said a lot about it, none of which he intended to go into at the moment. "So you don't know why she's here in Hungary?"

"I have no clue. Is she there with you now? Let me speak to her."

He flicked a glance at the woman sprawled across his bed. "She's zoned out, Sarah. Said she was tired and just flopped into bed."

"This memory thing? Will she be all right?"

"Like you, I have no clue. But you'd better contact her family just in case."

"She doesn't have any family."

"She's got to have someone. Grandparents? An uncle or aunt stashed away somewhere?"

"She doesn't," Sarah insisted. "Dev ran a detailed background check before I hired her. Natalie doesn't know who her parents are or why she was abandoned as an infant. She lived with a series of foster families until she checked herself out of the system at age eighteen and entered the University of Michigan on full scholarship."

That certainly put a different spin on the basic age-height-DOB info he'd gathered.

"I'll fly to Budapest immediately," Sarah was saying, "and take Natalie home with me until she recovers her memory."

Dom speared another glance at the researcher. His gut

told him he'd live to regret the suggestion he was about to make.

"Why don't you hang loose for now? Could be she'll be fine when she wakes up tomorrow. I'll call you then."

"I don't know…"

"I'll call you, Sarah. As soon as she wakes up."

When she reluctantly agreed, he cut the connection and stood with the phone in hand for several moments. He'd worked undercover too long to take anything at face value…especially a woman fished out of the Danube who had no reason to be in Budapest that anyone knew. Thumbing the phone, he tapped in a number. His contact at Interpol answered on the second ring.

"Oui?"

"It's Dom," he replied in swift, idiomatic French. "Remember the query you ran for me two weeks ago on Natalie Clark?"

"Oui."

"I need you to dig deeper."

"Oui."

The call completed, he contemplated his unexpected houseguest for a few moments. Her rumpled skirt had twisted around her calves and her buttoned-to-the-neck blouse looked as though it was choking her. After a brief inner debate, Dom rolled her over. He had the blouse unfastened and was easing it off when she opened her eyes to a groggy squint and mumbled at him.

"Whatryoudoin?"

"Making you comfortable."

"Mmm."

She was asleep again before he got her out of her blouse and skirt. Her panties were plain, unadorned white cotton but, Dom discovered, covered slender hips and a nice, trim butt. Nobly, he resisted the urge to remove her underwear and merely tucked the sheets around her. That done, he popped the cap on a bottle of a pilsner for himself, opened another for the hound and settled in for an all-night vigil.

He rolled her over again just after midnight and pried up a lid. She gave a bad-tempered grunt and batted his hand away, but not before he saw her pupil dilate and refract with reassuring swiftness.

He woke her again two hours later. "Natalie. Can you hear me?"

"Go away."

He did a final check just before dawn. Then he stretched out on the leather sofa and watched the dark night shade to gold and pink.

Something wet and cold prodded her elbow. Her shoulder. Her chin. She didn't come awake, though, until a strap of rough leather rasped across her cheek. She blinked fuzzily, registered the hazy thought that she was in bed, and opened her eyes.

"Yikes!"

A glistening pink mouth loomed only inches from her eyes. Its black gums were pulled back and a long tongue dangled through a set of nasty-looking incisors. As if in answer to her startled yip, the gaping mouth emitted a blast of powerful breath and an ear-ringing bark.

She scurried back like a poked crab, heart thumping and sheets tangling. A few feet of separation gave her a better perspective. Enough to see the merry eyes above an elongated muzzle, a broad forehead topped with one brown ear and one white, and a long, lean body with a wildly whipping tail.

Evidently the dog mistook her retreat for the notion that she was making space for him in the bed. With another loud woof, he landed on the mattress. The tongue went to work again, slathering her cheeks and chin before she could hold him off.

"Whoa! Stop!" His joy was contagious and as impossible to contain as his ecstatically wriggling body. Laughing now, she finally got him by the shoulders. "Okay, okay, I like you, too! But enough with the tongue."

He got in another slurp before he let her roll him onto his back, where he promptly stuck all four legs into the air and begged for a tickle. She complied and raised quivers of ecstasy on his short-haired ribs and speckled pink-and-brown belly.

"You're a handsome fellow," she murmured, admiring his sleek lines as her busy fingers set his legs to pumping. "Wonder what your name is?"

"He doesn't have one."

The response came from behind her. Twisting on the bed, she swept her startled gaze across a huge, sparsely furnished area. A series of overhead beams topped with A-frame wooden trusses suggested it was an attic. A stunningly renovated attic, with gleaming oak floors and modern lighting.

There were no interior walls, only a curved, waist-high counter made of glass blocks that partitioned off a kitchen area. The male behind the counter looked at home there. Dark-haired and dark-eyed, he wore a soccer shirt of brilliant red-and-black stripes with some team logo she didn't recognize emblazoned on one breast. The stretchy fabric molded his broad, muscular shoulders. The wavy glass blocks gave an indistinct view of equally muscular thighs encased in running shorts.

She watched him, her hand now stilled on the dog's belly, while he flicked the switch on a stainless-steel espresso machine. Almost instantly the machine hissed out thick, black liquid. Her eyes never left him as he filled two cups and rounded the glass-block counter.

When he crossed the huge room, the dog scrambled to sit up at his approach. So did she, tugging the sheet up with her. For some reason she couldn't quite grasp, she'd slept in her underwear.

He issued an order in a language she didn't understand. When he repeated it in a firmer voice, the dog jumped off the bed with obvious reluctance.

"How do you feel?"

"I…uh… Okay."

"Head hurt?"

She tried a tentative neck roll. "I don't… Ooh!"

Wincing, she fingered the lump at the base of her skull. "What happened?"

"Best guess is you fell off a bridge or tour boat and hit your head. Want some aspirin?"

"God, yes!"

He handed her one of the cups and crossed to what she guessed was a bathroom tucked under one of the eaves. She used his brief absence to let her gaze sweep the cavernous room again, looking for something, *anything* familiar.

Panic crawled like tiny ants down her spine when she finally accepted that she was sitting cross-legged on an unmade bed. In a strange apartment. With a hound lolling a few feet away, grinning from ear to ear and looking all too ready to jump back in with her.

Her hands shaking, she lifted the china cup. The rim rattled against her teeth and the froth coated her upper lip as she took a tentative sip.

"Ugh!"

Her first impulse was to spit the incredibly strong espresso back into the cup. Politeness—and the cool, watchful eyes of the bearer of aspirin—forced her to swallow.

"Better take these with water."

Gratefully, she traded the cup for a glass. She was

reaching for the two small white pills in his palm when she suddenly froze. Her heart slamming against her chest, she stared down at the pills.

Oh, God! Had she been drugged? Did he intend to knock her out again?

A faint thread of common sense tried to push through her balled-up nerves. If he wanted to drug her, he could just as easily have put something in her coffee. Still, she pulled her hand back.

"I...I better not. I, uh, may be allergic."

"You're not wearing a medical alert bracelet."

"I'm not wearing much of anything."

"True."

He set the pills and her cup on a low bookshelf that doubled as a nightstand. She clutched the water glass, looked at him, at the grinning dog, at the rumpled sheets, back at him. Ants started down her spine again.

"Okay," she said on a low, shaky breath, "who *are* you?

Four

"I'm Dominic. Dominic St. Sebastian. Dom to my friends and family."

He kept his eyes on her, watching for the tiniest flicker of recognition. If she was faking that blank stare, she was damned good at it.

"I'm Sarah's cousin," he added.

Nothing. Not a blink. Not a frown.

"Sarah St. Sebastian Hunter?" He waited a beat, then decided to go for the big guns. "She's the granddaughter of Charlotte, Grand Duchess of Karlenburgh."

"Karlenburgh?"

"You were researching a document pertaining to Karlenburgh. One with a special codicil."

He thought for a moment he'd struck a chord. Her brows drew together, and her lips bunched in an all-too-familiar moue. Then she blew out a breath and scooted to the edge of the bed, pulling the sheet with her.

"I don't know you, or your cousin, or her grandmother. Now, if you don't mind, I'd like to get dressed and be on my way."

"On your way to where?"

That brought her up short.

"I...I don't know." She blinked, obviously coming up empty. "Where...? Where am I?"

"Maybe this will help."

Dom went to the window and drew the drapes. Morning light flooded the loft. With it came the eagle's-eye view of the Danube and the Parliament's iconic red dome and forest of spires.

"Ooooh!" Wrapping the sheet around her like a sari, she stepped to the glass wall. "How glorious!"

"Do you recognize the building?"

"Sort of. Maybe."

She sounded anything but sure. And, Dom noted, she didn't squint or strain as she studied the elaborate structure across the river. Apparently she only needed her glasses for reading or close work. Yet...she'd worn them during both their previous meetings. Almost like a shield.

"I give up." She turned to him, those delicate nostrils quivering and panic clouding her eyes. "Where *am* I?"

"Budapest"

"Hungary?"

He started to ask if there was a city with that same name in another country but the panic had started to spill over into tears. Although she tried valiantly to gulp them back, she looked so frightened and fragile that Dom had to take her in his arms.

The sobs came then. Big, noisy gulps that brought the Agár leaping to all fours. His ears went flat and his long, narrow tail whipped out, as though he sensed an enemy but wasn't sure where to point.

"It's all right," Dom said, as much to the dog as the woman in his arms. She smelled of the river, he thought as he stroked her hair. The river and diesel spill and soft, trembling female still warm from his bed. So different from the stiff, disdainful woman who'd ordered him out of her New York hotel room that his voice dropped to a husky murmur.

"It's all right."

"No, it's not!"

The tears gushed now, soaking through his soccer shirt and making the dog whine nervously. His claws clicked on the oak planking as he circled Dom and the woman clinging to his shirt with one hand and the sheet with her other.

"I don't understand any of this! Why can't I remember where I am? Why can't I remember *you*?" She jerked back against his arm and stared up at him. "Are we...? Are we married?"

"No."

Her glance shot to the bed. "Lovers?"

He let that hang for a few seconds before treating her to a slow smile.

"Not yet."

Guilt pricked at him then. Her eyes were so huge and frightened, her nose red and sniffling. Gentling his voice, he brushed a thumb across her cheek to wipe the tears.

"Do you remember the police bringing you here last night?"

"I...I think so."

"They took you to a hospital first. Remember?"

Her forehead wrinkled. "Now I do."

"A doctor examined you. He told the police that short-term memory loss isn't unusual with a head injury."

She jumped on that. "How short?"

"I don't know, *drágám*."

"Is that my name? *Drágám*?"

"No, that's a nickname. An endearment, like 'sweetheart' or 'darling.' Very casual here in Hungary," he added when her eyes got worried again. "Your name is Natalie. Natalie Elizabeth Clark."

"Natalie." She rolled it around in her head, on her tongue. "Not a name I would pick for myself," she said with a sniffle, "but I guess it'll do."

The brown-and-white hound poked at her knee then, as if demanding reassurance that all was well. Natalie eased out of Dom's arms and knuckled the dog's broad, intelligent forehead.

"And who's this guy?"

"I call him *kutya*. It means 'dog' in Hungarian."

Her eyes lifted to his, still watery but accusing. "You just call him 'dog'?"

"He followed me home one night and decided to take up residence. I thought it would be a temporary arrangement, so we never got around to a baptismal ceremony."

"So he's a stray," she murmured, her voice thickening. "Like me."

Dom knew he'd better act fast to head off another storm of tears. "Stray or not," he said briskly, "he needs to go out. Why don't you shower and finish your coffee while I take him for his morning run? I'll pick up some apple pancakes for breakfast while I'm out, yes? Then we'll talk about what to do next."

When she hesitated, her mouth trembling, he curled a knuckle under her chin and tipped her face to his. "We'll work this out, Natalie. Let's just take it one step at a time."

She bit her lip and managed a small nod.

"Your clothes are in the bathroom," Dom told her. "I rinsed them out last night, but they're probably still damp." He nodded to the double-doored wardrobe positioned close to the bath. "Help yourself to whatever you can find to fit you."

She nodded again and hitched the sheet higher to keep from tripping over it as she padded to the bathroom. Dom waited until he heard the shower kick on before dropping into a chair to pull on socks and his well-worn running shoes.

He hoped to hell he wasn't making a mistake leaving her alone. Short of locking her in, though, he didn't see how he could confine her here against her will. Besides which, they needed to eat and Dog needed to go out. A point the hound drove home by retrieving his leash from its hook by the door and waiting with an expression of acute impatience.

Natalie. Natalie Elizabeth Clark.

Why didn't it feel right? Sound right?

She wrapped her freshly shampooed hair in a towel and stared at the steamed-up bathroom mirror. The image it reflected was as foggy as her mind.

She'd stood under the shower's hot, driving needles and tried to figure out what in the world she was doing in Budapest. It couldn't be her home. She didn't know a word of Hungarian. Correction. She knew two. *Kutya* and... What had he called her? *Dragon* or something.

Dominic. His name was Dominic. It fit him, she thought with a grimace, much better than Natalie did her. Those muscled shoulders, the strong arms, the chest she'd sobbed against, all hinted at power and virility and, yes, dominance.

Especially in bed. The thought slipped in, got caught in her mind. He'd said they weren't lovers. Implied she'd slept alone. Yet heat danced in her belly at the thought of lying beneath him and feeling his hands on her breasts, his mouth on her...

Oh, God! The panic came screaming back. She breathed in. Out. In. Then set her jaw and glared at the face in the mirror.

"No more crying! It didn't help before! It won't help now."

She snatched up a dry washcloth and had started to scrub the fogged glass when she caught the echo of her words. Her fist closed around the cloth, and her chest squeezed.

"Crying didn't help before *what*?"

Like the steam still drifting from the shower stall,

the mists in her mind seemed to curl. Shift. Become less
opaque. Something was there, just behind the thin gray
curtain. She could almost see it. Almost smell it. She spun
around and hacked out a sound halfway between a sob
and a laugh.

She could smell it, all right. The musty odor emanated
from the wrinkled items hanging from hooks on the door.
The steam from the hot shower must have released the
river stink.

Her nose wrinkling, she fingered the shapeless jacket,
the unadorned blouse, the mess that must once have been
a skirt. Good grief! Were these really her clothes? They
looked like they'd come from a Goodwill grab bag. The bra
and panties she'd discarded before getting in the shower
were even worse.

He—Dominic—said he'd rinsed her things out. He
should have tossed them in a garbage sack and hauled
them to a dumpster.

"Well," she said with a shrug, "he told me to help myself."

The helping included using his comb to work the tangles
from her wet hair and squirting a length of his toothpaste
onto her forefinger to scrub her teeth. It also included poking her head through the bathroom door to make sure he
was still gone before she raided his closet.

It was a European-style wardrobe, with mirror double
doors and beautiful carving. The modern evolution of the
special room in a castle where nobles stored their robes
in carved wooden chests. Called an armoire in French,
a shrunk in German, this particular wardrobe wasn't as
elaborate as some she'd seen but...

Wait! How did she know about castles and nobles and
shrunks? What other, more elaborate armoires had she
seen? She stared at the hunting scene above the doors,

feeling as though she was straining every brain cell she possessed through a sieve, and came up empty.

"Dammit!"

Angry and more than a little scared, she yanked open the left door. Suits and dress shirts hung haphazardly from the rod, while an assortment of jeans, T-shirts and sporting gear spilled from the shelves below. She plucked out a soccer shirt, this one with royal-blue and white stripes but with the same green-and-gold emblem on the right sleeve. The cool, slick material slithered over her hips. The hem hung almost to her knees.

Curiosity prompted her to open the right door. This side was all drawers. The top drawer contained unmatched socks, tangled belts, loose change and a flashlight.

The middle drawer was locked. Securely locked, with a gleaming steel mechanism that didn't give a hair when she tested it.

She slid the third drawer out and eyed the jumble of jock straps, Speedos and boxers. She thought about appropriating a Speedo but couldn't quite bring herself to climb into his underwear.

"Not the neatest guy in the world, are you?" she commented to the absent Dominic.

She started to close the drawer, intending to go back to the bathroom and give her panties a good scrubbing, when she caught a glimpse of delicate black lace amid boxers.

Oh, Lord! Was he into kink? Cross-dressing? Transgender sex play? Did that locked drawer contain whips and handcuffs and ball gags?

She gulped, remembering her earlier thought about strength and power and dominance, and used the tip of a finger to extract a pair of lace-trimmed silk hipsters. A new and very expensive pair of hipsters judging by the embossed tag still dangling from the band. Natalie's eyes widened when she saw the hand-lettered price.

Good grief! Three hundred pounds? Could that be right?

When she recovered from sticker shock, she found it interesting that the price was displayed in British pounds and not in Hungarian…Hungarian whatever. Also interesting, the light-as-air scrap of silk had evidently been crafted by an "atelier" who described her collection as feminine and ethereal, each piece a limited edition made to measure for the client. The matching garter belt and triangle bra, the tag advised, would put the cost for the complete ensemble at just over a thousand pounds.

Well, she thought with a low whistle, if he was into kink, he certainly did it up right. She was about to stuff the panties back in the drawer when she noticed handwriting on the back of the tag.

I stuck these in your suitcase so you'll know what I won't be wearing next time you're in London.
Kiss, kiss, Arabella.

Oh, yuck! Her lip curling, she started to stuff the hipsters back in the drawer. Common sense and a bare butt made her hesitate several seconds too long. She still had the panties in hand when the front door opened and the hound burst in. Sweat darkened the honey-brown patches on the dog's coat. Similar damp splotches stained Dominic's soccer shirt.

"Find everything you need?" he asked as he dropped a leash and a white paper sack on the kitchen counter.

"Almost everything." She lifted her hand. The scrap of silk and lace dangled from her forefinger. "Do you think Arabella will mind if I borrow her knickers?"

"Who?"

"Arabella. London. Kiss, kiss."

"Oh. Right. That Arabella." He eyed the gossamer silk

with a waggle of his brow. "Very nice. Where'd you find them?"

"In with your socks," she drawled. "There's a note on the back of the tag."

He flipped the tag over and skimmed the handwriting. She could smell the sharp tang of his sweat, see the bristles darkening his cheeks and chin. See, too, the smile that played at the corners of his mouth. He managed to keep it from sliding into a full grin as he handed back the panties.

"I'm sure Arabella wouldn't mind you borrowing them," he said solemnly.

But *he* would. The realization hit Dom even before she whirled and the hem of his soccer shirt flared just high enough to give him a glimpse of her nicely curved butt.

"That might have been a mistake," he told the hound when the bathroom door shut. "Now I'm going to be imagining her in black silk all day."

The Agár cocked his head. The brown ear came up, the white ear folded over, and he looked as though he was giving the matter serious consideration.

"She's fragile," Dom reminded the dog sternly. "Confused and frightened and probably still hurting from her dive into the Danube. So you refrain from slobbering all over her front and I'll keep my mind off her rear."

Easier said than done he discovered when she re-emerged. She wore a cool expression, the blue crew shirt and, as Dom could all-too-easily visualize, a band of black silk around her slender hips.

And here he'd thought her nondescript back in New York. She certainly looked different with her face flushed and rosy from the shower and her damp hair showing streaks of rich, dark chestnut. The oversize glasses had dominated her face in New York, distracting from those cinnamon-brown eyes and the short, straight nose. And, he remembered, her full lips had been set in such thin, disapproving lines for most of their brief acquaintance. They were close to that now but still looked very kissable.

Not that he should be thinking about her eyes or her lips or the length of bare leg visible below the hem of his shirt. She's vulnerable, he had to remember. Confused.

"I bought some apple pancakes from my favorite street seller," he told her, indicating the white sack on the counter. "They're good cold, if you're hungry now, but better when crisped a bit in the oven. Help yourself while I take my turn in the shower."

"I'll warm them up."

Rounding the glass counter, she stooped to study the knobs on the stovetop. The soccer shirt rode up again. Barely an inch. Two at the most. All it showed were the backs of her thighs, but Dom had to swallow a groan as he grabbed a pair of jeans and a clean shirt and hit the bathroom.

He didn't take long. A hot, stinging shower and a quick shampoo. He scraped a palm over his three or four days' worth of bristles, but a shave lost out to the seductive scent of warm apples.

She was perched on one of the counter stools, laughing at the shivering bundle of ecstasy hunkered between her bare legs. "No, you idiot! Don't give me that silly grin. I'm not feeding you another bite."

She glanced up, her face still alight, and spotted Dom. The laughter faded instantly. He felt the loss like a hard right jab to the solar plexus.

Jézus, Mária és József! Did she dislike all men, or just him? He couldn't tell but sure as hell intended to find out.

The woman represented so many mysteries. There was the disdain she'd treated him to in New York. That ridiculous codicil. The memory loss. The yet-to-be-explained reason she was here in his loft, swathed in his soccer shirt. Dom couldn't remember when a woman had challenged him in so many ways. He was about to tell her so when the cell phone he'd left on the counter buzzed.

"It's Sarah," he said after a quick glance at the face that came up on the screen. "My cousin and your boss. Do you want to talk to her?"

"I…uh… All right."

He accepted the FaceTime call and gave his anxious cousin the promised update. "Natalie's still here with me. Physically she seems okay but no progress yet on recovering her memory. Here, I'll put her on."

He positioned the phone so the screen captured Natalie still seated on the high stool. Both he and Sarah could see the desperate hope and crushing disappointment that chased across the researcher's features as she stared at the face on the screen.

"Oh, Nat," Sarah said with a tremulous smile, "I'm so, so sorry to hear you've been hurt."

Her hand crept to her nape. "Thank you."

"Dev and I will fly to Budapest today and take you home."

Uncertainty flooded her eyes. "Dev?"

Sarah swallowed. "Devon Hunter. My husband."

The name didn't appear to register, which caused Natalie such obvious dismay that Dom intervened. Leaning close, he spoke into the camera.

"Why don't you and Dev hold off for a while, Sarah? We haven't spoken to the police yet this morning. They were going to trace Natalie's movements in Hungary and might have some information for us. Also, they might have found her purse or briefcase. If not, we'll need to go to the American Embassy and get a replacement passport before she can leave the country. That could take a few days."

"But…"

Sarah struggled to mask her concern. Dom guessed she felt personally responsible for her assistant being hurt and stranded in a foreign country.

"Are you good with remaining in Hungary a little while yet, Nat?"

"I…" She looked from the screen to Dom to the hound, who now sat with his head plopped on her knee. "Yes."

"Would you feel better staying at a hotel? I can make a reservation in your name today."

Once again Dom felt compelled to intercede. Natalie was in no condition to be left on her own. Assuming, of course, her memory loss was real. He had no reason to believe otherwise but the cop in him went too deep to take anyone or anything at face value.

"Let's leave that for now, too," he told Sarah. "As I said, we need to talk to the police and start the paperwork for a replacement passport if necessary. While we're working things at this end, you could make some inquiries back in the States. Talk to the duchess and Zia and Gina. Maybe the editor you're working with on your book. Find out if anyone's called inquiring about Natalie or her research. It might help jog her memory if we can discover what brought her to Budapest from Vienna."

"Of course. I'll do that today." She hesitated, clearly distressed for her assistant. "You'll need money, Natalie. I'll arrange a draft… No, we'd better make it cash since you don't have any ID. I'll have it delivered to Dom's address this afternoon. Just an advance on your salary," she added quickly when Natalie looked as though she'd been offered charity.

Dom considered telling his cousin that the money could wait, too. He was more than capable of covering his unexpected guest's expenses. More to the point, it might be better to keep her dependent on him until they sorted out her situation. On reflection, though, he decided the leash was short enough.

The brief conversation left Natalie silent for several long moments. She scratched the hound's head, obviously dismayed over not recognizing the woman she worked for and with. Dom moved quickly to head off another possible panic attack.

"Okay, here's today's agenda," he said with brisk cheerfulness. "First, we finish breakfast. Second, we hit the shops to buy you some shoes and whatever else you need. Third, we visit police headquarters to find out what, if anything, they've learned. We also get a copy of their incident report and contact the embassy to begin the paperwork for a replacement passport. Finally, and most important, we arrange a follow-up with the doctor you saw yesterday. Or better yet, with a specialist who has some expertise dealing with amnesia cases."

"Sounds good to me," she said, relief at having a concrete plan of action edging aside the dismay. "But do you really think we can swing an appointment with a specialist anytime soon? Or even find one with expertise in amnesia?"

"I've got a friend I can call."

He didn't tell her that his "friend" was the internationally renowned forensic pathologist who'd autopsied the victims of a particularly savage drug cartel last year. Dom had witnessed each autopsy, groaning at the doc's morbid sense of humor as he collected the evidence Interpol needed to take down key members of the cartel.

He made the call while Natalie conducted another raid on his wardrobe. By the time she'd dug out a pair of Dom's flip-flops and running shorts with a drawstring waist, one of Budapest's foremost neurologists had agreed to squeeze her in at 11:20 a.m.

Five

The short-notice appointment with the neurologist necessitated a quick change in the day's agenda. Almost before Natalie had downed her last bite of apple pancake, Dom hustled her to the door of the loft and down five flights of stairs to the underground garage.

It'd been dark when she'd arrived the previous evening, so she'd caught only glimpses of the castle dominating the hill on the Buda of the river. The bright light of morning showed the royal palace in its full glory.

"Oh, look!" Her glance snagged on the bronze warrior atop a muscled warhorse that guarded the entrance to the castle complex. "That's Prince Eugene of Savoy, isn't it?"

Dominic slanted her a quick look. "You know about *Priz Eugen*?"

"Of course." She twisted in her seat to keep the statue in view as they negotiated the narrow, curving streets that would take them down to the Danube. "He was one of the greatest military leaders of the seventeenth century. As I recall, he served three different Holy Roman Emperors and won a decisive victory against the Ottoman Turks in 1697 at…"

She broke off, her eyes rounding. "Why do I know that?"

She sank back against her seat and stared through the windshield at the tree-dappled street ahead. Dom said nothing while she struggled to jam together the pieces of the puzzle.

"Why do I know the Hapsburgs built this palace on the site of the Gothic castle originally constructed by an earlier Holy Roman Emperor? Why do I know it was reconstructed after being razed to the ground during World War II?" Her fists bunched, drummed her thighs. "Why can I pull those details out of my head and not know who I am or how I ended up in the river?"

"Recalling those details has to be a good sign. Maybe it means you'll start to remember other things, as well."

"God, I hope so!"

Her fists stayed tight through the remainder of the descent from Castle Hill and across the majestic Chain Bridge linking Buda and Pest.

Their first stop was a small boutique, where Natalie traded Dom's drawstring shorts, soccer shirt and flip-flops for sandals, slim designer jeans, a cap-sleeved tank in soft peach and a straw tote. A second stop garnered a few basic toiletries. Promising to shop for other necessities later, Dom hustled her back to the car for her appointment with Dr. Andras Kovacs.

The neurologist's suite of offices occupied the second floor of a gracious nineteenth-century town house in the shadow of St. Stephen's Basilica. The gray-haired receptionist in the outer office confirmed Natalie's short-notice appointment, but showed more interest in her escort than the patient herself.

"I read about you in the paper," she exclaimed to Dom in Hungarian. "Aren't you the Grand Duke of...of...something?"

Swallowing a groan, he nodded. "Of Karlenburgh, but the title is an empty one. The duchy doesn't exist any longer."

"Still, it must be very exciting to suddenly find yourself a duke."

"Yes, very. Is Dr. Kovacs running on time for his appointments?"

"He is." She beamed. "Please have a seat, Your Highness, and I'll let his assistant know you and Ms. Clark are here."

When he led Natalie to a set of tall wingback chairs, she sent him a quick frown. "What was all that about?"

"She was telling me about a story she'd read in the paper."

"I heard her say 'Karlenburgh.'"

He eyed her closely. "Do you recognize that name?"

"You mentioned it this morning. I thought for a moment I knew it." Still frowning, she scrubbed her forehead with the heel of her hand. "It's all here, somewhere in my head. That name. That place. You."

Her eyes lifted to his. She looked so accusing, he had to smile.

"I can think of worse places to be than in your head, *drágám.*"

He wasn't sure whether it was the lazy smile or the casual endearment or the husky note to his voice that brought out the Natalie Clark he'd met in New York. Whatever the reason, she responded with a hint of her old, disapproving self.

"You shouldn't call me that. I'm not your sweetheart."

He couldn't help himself. Lifting a hand, he brushed a knuckle over the curve of her cheek. "Ah, but we can change that, yes?"

She pulled away, and Dom was cursing himself for the mix of wariness and confusion that came back to her face when a slim, thirtysomething woman in a white smock coat emerged from the inner sanctum.

"Ms. Clark? I'm Dr. Kovacs's assistant," she said in Hungarian. "Would you and your husband please follow me?"

"Ms. Clark is American," Dom told her. "She doesn't speak our language. And we're not married."

"Oh, my apologies."

Switching to English, she repeated the invitation and advised Natalie it was her choice whether she wished to have her friend join her for the consult. Dom half expected her to refuse but she surprised him.

"I'd better have someone with me who knows who I am."

The PA showed them to a consultation room lined with mahogany bookshelves displaying leather-bound volumes and marble busts. No desk, just high-backed wing chairs in Moroccan leather arranged around a marble-topped pedestal table. The physician fit his surroundings. Tall and lean, he boasted an aristocratic beak of a nose and kind eyes behind rimless glasses.

"I reviewed the computer results of your examination at the hospital yesterday," he told Natalie in flawless English. "I would have preferred a complete physical exam with diagnostic imaging and cognitive testing before consulting with you, of course. Despite the limited medical data available at this point, however, I doubt your memory loss resulted from an organic issue such as a stroke or brain tumor or dementia. That's the good news."

Natalie's breath hissed softly on the air. The sound made Dom reach for her hand.

"What's the bad?" she asked, her fingers closing around his.

"Despite what you see in movies and on television, Ms. Clark, it's very rare for persons suffering from amnestic syndrome to lose their self-identity. A head injury such as the one you sustained generally leads to confusion and problems remembering *new* information, not old."

"I'm starting to remember things." Her fingers curled tighter, the nails digging into Dom's palm. "Historical dates and facts and such."

"Good, that's good. But for you to have blocked your sense of self…"

Kovacs slid his rimless glasses to the tip of his nose. Dom found himself wondering again about Natalie's glasses, but pushed the thought to the back of his mind as the doctor continued.

"There's another syndrome. It's called psychogenic, or dissociative, amnesia. It can result from emotional shock or trauma, such as being a victim of rape or some other violent crime."

"I don't think…" Her nails gouged deeper, sharper. "I don't remember any…"

"The hospital didn't run a rape kit," Dom said when she stumbled to a halt. "There was no reason to. Natalie—Ms. Clark—doesn't have any defensive wounds or bruises other than the swelling at the base of her skull."

"I'm aware of that. And I'm not suggesting the trauma is necessarily recent. It could have happened weeks or months or years ago." He turned back to Natalie. "The blow to your head may have triggered a memory of some previous painful experience. Perhaps caused you to throw up a defensive shield and block all personal memories."

"Will…" She swiped her tongue over her lower lip. "Will these personal memories come back?"

"They do in most instances. Each case is so different, however, it's impossible to predict a pattern."

Her jaw set. "So how do I pry open Pandora's box? Are there drugs I should take? Mental exercises I can do?"

"For now, I suggest you just give it a little time. You're a visitor to Budapest, yes? Soak in the baths. Enjoy the opera. Stroll in our beautiful parks. Let your mind heal along with the injury to your head."

The neurologist's parting advice didn't sit well with Natalie.

"Hit the opera," she huffed as they exited the town house. "Soak in the baths. Easy for him to say!"

"And easy for us to do."

The drawled comment brought her up short. Coming to a dead stop in the middle of the wide, tree-shaded sidewalk, she cocked her head.

"How can you dawdle around Budapest with me? Don't you have a job? An office or a brickyard or a butcher shop wondering where you are?"

"I wish I worked in a butcher shop," he replied, laughing. "I could keep the hound in bones for the rest of his life."

"Don't dodge the question. Where do you work?"

"Nowhere at the moment, thanks to you."

"Me?" A dozen wild possibilities raced through her head but none of them made any sense. "I don't understand."

"No, I don't suppose you do." He hooked a hand under her elbow and steered her toward a café a short distance away. "Come, let's have a coffee and I'll explain."

If Budapest's many thermal springs and public baths had made it a favorite European spa destination since Roman times, the city owed its centuries-old café culture to the Turks. Suleyman the Magnificent first introduced coffee to Europe when he invaded Hungary in the 1500s.

Taste for the drink grew during the Austro-Hungarian Empire. Meeting friends for coffee or just claiming a table to linger over a book or newspaper became a time-honored tradition. Although Vienna and other European cities developed their own thriving café cultures, Budapest remained its epicenter and at one time boasted more than six hundred *kávébáz*.

Hungarians still loved to gather at cafés. Most were small places with a dozen or so marble-topped tables, serving the inevitable glass of water along with a pitcher of milk and a cup of coffee on a small silver tray. But a few of the more elegant nineteenth-century cafés still remained. The one Dom escorted Natalie to featured chandeliers dripping with Bohemian crystal and a monstrous brass coffeemaker that took up almost one whole wall.

They claimed an outside table shaded by a green-and-white-striped awning. Dom placed the order, and Natalie waited only until they'd both stirred milk and sugar into their cups to pounce.

"All right. Please explain why I'm responsible for you being currently unemployed."

"You uncovered a document in some dusty archives in Vienna. A codicil to the Edict of 1867, which granted certain rights to Hungarian nobles. The codicil specifically confirmed the title of Grand Duke of Karlenburgh to the house of St. Sebastian forever and in perpetuity. Does any of this strike a chord?"

"That name. Karlenburgh. I know I know it."

"It was a small duchy, not much larger than Monaco, that straddled the present-day border between Austria and Hungary. The Alps cut right through it. Even today it's a place of snow-capped peaks, fertile valleys and high mountain passes guarded by crumbling fortresses."

"You've been there?"

"Several times. My grandfather was born at Karlenburgh Castle. It's just a pile of rubble now, but Poppa took my parents, then my sister and me back to see it."

"Your grandfather was the Grand Duke?"

"No, that was Sarah's grandfather. Mine was his cousin." Dom hesitated, thinking about the blood ties that had so recently and dramatically turned his life upside down. "I suppose my grandfather could have tried to claim the title when the last Grand Duke was executed."

He stirred his coffee again and tried to imagine those long ago days of terror and chaos.

"From what he told me, that was a brutal time. The Soviet invasion leveled everyone—or elevated them, depending on how you looked at it—to the status of comrade. Wealth and titles became dangerous liabilities and made their holders targets. People tried to flee to the West. Neighbors spied on neighbors. Then, after the 1956 Uprising, the KGB rounded up thousands of nationalists. Charlotte, Sarah's grandmother, was forced to witness her husband's execution, and barely escaped Hungary with her life."

The history resonated somewhere in Natalie's mind. She'd heard this story before. She knew she had. She just didn't know how it connected her and the broad-shouldered man sitting across from her.

"So this dusty document you say I uncovered? It links you to the title?"

"Charlotte thinks it does. So, unfortunately, do the tabloids." His mouth twisted. "They've been hounding me since news of that damned document surfaced."

"Well, excuse me for making you aware of your heritage!"

His brows soared. He stared at her with such an arrested expression that she had to ask.

"What?"

"You said almost the same thing in New York. While you were tearing off a strip of my hide."

The revelation that she'd taken him down a peg or two did wonders for her self-confidence. "I'm sure you deserved it," she said primly.

This time he just laughed.

"What?" she demanded again.

"That's you, *drágám*. So proper. So prissy. That's the Natalie who made me ache to tumble her to the bed or a sofa and kiss the disapproval from those luscious lips. I hurt for an hour after I left you in New York."

Her jaw dropped. She couldn't speak. Could barely breathe. Some distant corner of her mind warned that she would lose, and lose badly, if she engaged Dominic St. Sebastian in an exchange of sexual repartee.

Yet she couldn't seem to stop herself. Forcing a provocative smile, she leaned her elbows on the table and dropped her voice to the same husky murmur Dom had employed in Dr. Kovacs's reception area.

"Ah, but we can fix that, yes?"

His blank astonishment shot her ego up another notch. For the first time since she'd come awake and found herself eye to eye with a grinning canine, Natalie was able to shelve her worry and confusion.

The arrival of a waiter with their lunch allowed her to revel in the sensation awhile longer. Only after she'd forked down several bites of leafy greens and crunchy cucumber did she return to their original topic.

"You still haven't explained how inheriting the title associated with a long-defunct duchy put you on the rolls of the unemployed."

He swept the café with a casual glance. So casual she didn't realize he was making sure no one was close enough to overhear until he delivered another jaw-dropper.

"I'm an undercover agent, Natalie. Or I was until all this Grand Duke business hit."

"Like...?" She tried to get her head around it. "Like James Bond or something?"

"Closer to something. After my face got splashed across the tabloids, my boss encouraged me to take a nice, long vacation."

"So that explains the drawer!"

He leaned back in his chair. Slowly. Too slowly. Although the September sun warmed the cozy space under the awning and the exhaust from the cabs clogging the boulevard shimmered on the afternoon air, Natalie had the eerie sensation that the temperature around their table had dropped at least ten degrees.

"What drawer?"

"The locked one in your wardrobe. You store all your 007-type gadgets in there, don't you? Poison pens and jet-propelled socks and laser-guided minimissiles?"

He didn't answer for several moments. When he did, her brief euphoria at being in control evaporated.

"This isn't about me, Nat. You're the one with the empty spaces that need filling. Let's finish our coffee, yes? Then we'll swing by police headquarters. With any luck, they will have found the answers to at least some of your questions."

Dom called before they left the café to make sure Officer Gradjnic, his partner or their supervisor would be available to speak with them. Natalie didn't say a word during the short drive. Budapest traffic was nerve-racking enough to tie anyone in knots. The possibility that the police might lift a corner of the curtain blanketing her mind only added to her twist of nerves.

The National Police Department occupied a multistory, glass-and-steel high-rise on the Pest side of the Danube. Command and control of nationwide operations filled the upper stories. The Budapest PD claimed the first two floors. Officer Gradjnic's precinct was crammed into a corner of the second floor.

Natalie remembered Gradjnic from yesterday. More or less. Enough to smile when he asked how she was feeling, anyway, and thank him for their help yesterday.

"So, Ms. Clark. Do you remember how you ended up in the Danube?"

"No."

"But you might, yes?"

"The doctor we consulted this morning said that was possible." She swiped her tongue over suddenly dry lips. "What have you discovered?"

"A little."

Computers sat on every desk in the office but Officer Gradjnic tugged out his leather notepad, licked his finger and flipped through the pages.

"We've verified that you flew from Paris to Vienna last week," he reported. "We've also learned that you rented a vehicle from the Europcar agency in Vienna three days ago. We had the car rental company retrieve the GPS data from the vehicle and discovered you crossed into Hungary at Pradzéc."

"Where's Pradzéc?"

"It's a small village at the foot of the Alps, straddling the border between Austria and Hungary."

Her glance shot to Dom. They'd been talking about the border area less than an hour ago. He didn't so much as flick an eyelid but she knew he'd made the connection, just as she had.

"According to the GPS records, you spent several hours in that area, then returned to Vienna. The next day you crossed into Hungary again and stopped in Győr. The vehicle is still there, Ms. Clark, parked at a tour dock on the Danube. We called the tour office and verified that a woman matching your description purchased a ticket for a day cruise to Budapest. Do you recall buying that ticket, Ms. Clark?"

"No."

"Do you remember boarding the tour boat? Watching the scenery as you cruised down the Danube, perhaps?"

"No."

He shrugged and closed his notebook. "Well, that's all I have for you, I'm afraid. You'll have to make arrangements to return the rental car."

Dom nodded. "We'll take care of it. In the meantime, we'd like a copy of your report."

"Of course."

When they walked out into the afternoon sunshine, Natalie couldn't wait to ask. "Was Győr part of the duchy of Karlenburgh?"

"At one time."

"Is Karlenburgh Castle anywhere in that vicinity?"

"It's farther west, guarding a mountain pass. Or was. It's just a pile of ruins now."

"I need to retrace my steps, Dominic. Maybe if I see the ruins or the towns or the countryside I drove through, I'll remember why I was there."

"We'll go tomorrow."

A part of her cringed a bit at being so dependent on this man, who was still almost a stranger to her. Yet she couldn't help feeling relieved he would accompany her.

"We can have someone from Europcar meet us in Győr with a set of master keys," he advised. "That way you can retrieve any luggage you might have left locked in the trunk."

"Assuming it's still there. Rental cars are always such targets."

"True. Now we'd better see about getting you a replacement passport."

He pulled up the necessary information from the US Embassy's consular services on his iPhone. "As I thought. You'll need proof of US citizenship. A birth certificate, driver's license or previous passport."

"None of which I have."

"I can help there. I'll have one my contacts obtain a copy of your driver's license."

"You can do that?"

When he just smiled, she slapped the heel of her hand against her forehead. "Of course you can. You're 007."

They walked to the car and he opened the passenger door for her. Before she slid into the seat, Natalie turned. "You're a man of many different personas, Dominic St. Sebastian. Grand Duke. Secret agent. Rescuer of damsels in distress."

His mouth curved. "Of the three, I enjoy the last most."

"Hmm." He was so close, almost caging her in, that she had to tip her chin to look up at him. "That comes naturally to you, doesn't it?"

"Rescuing damsels in distress?"

"No, that slow, sexy, let's-get-naked grin."

"Is that the message it sends?"

"Yes."

"Is it working?"

She pursed her lips. "No."

"Ah, *drágám*," he said, laughter springing into his eyes, "every time you do that, I want to do this."

She sensed what was coming. Knew she should duck under his arm, drop into her seat and slam the door. Instead she stood there like an idiot while he stooped, placed his mouth over hers and kissed the disapproval off her lips.

Six

It was just a kiss. Nothing to get all jittery about. And certainly no reason for a purr to start deep in Natalie's throat and heat to ball in her belly. She could feel both, though, right along with the sensual movement of Dominic's lips over hers.

She'd thought it would end there. One touch. One pass of his mouth over hers. It *should* have ended there. Traffic was coursing along the busy street, for pity's sake. A streetcar clanged by. Yet Natalie didn't move as his arm went around her waist, drawing her closer, while her pulse pounded in her veins.

She was breathing hard when Dominic raised his head. He was, too, but recovered much quicker than she did.

"There," he teased. "That's better. You don't want to walk around with your mouth all pruned up."

She couldn't think of an appropriate response, so she merely sniffed and ducked into the car.

She struggled to regain her equilibrium as the car negotiated the narrow, winding streets of Castle Hill. Yet with every turn of the wheels she could feel Dominic's mouth on hers, still taste him.

She snuck a sideways glance, wondering if he was experiencing any aftershocks. No, of course not. He was supercool Mr. Secret Agent. Sexy Mr. Grand Duke, who had women slipping outrageously expensive panties into his carryall. The thought of him cuddling with Kissy Face Arabella struck a sour note in Natalie's mind. Not that it was any of her business *who* he cuddled with, she reminded herself sternly. She certainly had no claim on the man, other than being dropped on his doorstep like an abandoned baby.

That thought, in turn, triggered alternating ripples of worry and fear. She had to battle both emotions as Dom pulled into his parking space in the underground garage and they climbed the five flights of stairs. The enclosed stairwell blocked any glimpse of the river but it did afford a backside view of the uniformed delivery man trudging up ahead of them.

When they caught up with him at the landing outside the loft, Dom gestured to the large envelope in his hand. "Is that for me?"

"It is if you're Dominic St. Sebastian."

He signed for the delivery, noting the address of the sender. "It's from Sarah."

He pulled the tab on the outer envelope and handed Natalie the one inside. She fingered the bulging package before slipping it into her new straw tote. She didn't know the currency or the denomination of the notes her employer had sent but it felt like a fat wad. More than enough, she was sure, to repay Dom for her new clothes and the consult with Dr. Kovacs.

The money provided an unexpected anchor in her drifting world. When Dom unlocked the door to the loft and stood aside for her to enter, the hound provided another. Delirious with joy at their return, he woofed and waggled and whirled in ecstatic circles.

"Okay, Dog, okay." Laughing, Natalie dropped to her knees and fondled his ears. "I missed you, too."

He got in a few quick licks on her cheeks and chin

before she could dodge them. The silly grin on his face tugged at her heart.

"You can't keep calling him 'Dog,'" she scolded Dom. "He needs a proper name."

"What do you suggest?"

She studied the animal's madly whipping tail and white coat with its saddle-brown markings. "He looks a lot like a greyhound, but he's not, is he?"

"There may be some greyhound in him but he's mostly Magyar Agár."

"Magyar Agár." She rolled the words around in her head but drew a blank. "I'm not familiar with that breed."

"They're long-distance-racing and hunting hounds. In the old days, they would run alongside horsemen, often for twenty miles or more, to take down fast game like deer or hare. Anyone could own one, but big fellows like this one normally belonged to royalty."

"Royalty, huh. That settles it." She gave the cropped ears another tug. "You have to call him Duke."

"No."

"It's perfect," she insisted with a wicked glint in her eyes.

"No, Natalie."

"Think of the fun you can have if some pesky reporter wants to interview the duke."

Even better, think of the fun *she* could have whistling and ordering him to heel. "What do you say?" she asked the hound. "Think you could live with a royal title?"

Her answer was an ear-rattling woof.

"There, that settles the matter." She rose and dusted her hands. "What happens to Duke here when you're off doing your James Bond thing?"

"There's a girl in the apartment downstairs who looks after him for me."

Of course there was. Probably another Arabella-From-

London type. Natalie could just imagine what kind of payment she demanded for her dog-sitting services.

The thought was small and nasty and not one she was proud of. She chalked it up to these bizarre circumstances and the fact that she could still feel the imprint of Dom's mouth on her.

"I'd better take his highness out," he said. "Do you want to walk with us?"

She did, but she couldn't get the memory of their kiss out of her head. It didn't help that Dom was leaning against the counter, looking at her with those bedroom eyes.

"You go ahead," she said, needing some time and space. As an excuse she held up the straw tote with its cache of newly purchased toiletries. "Do you mind if I put some of these things in your bathroom?"

"Be my guest, *drágám*."

"I asked you not to call me that."

Nerves and a spark of temper made her sound waspish even to her own ears. He noted the tone but shrugged it off.

"So you did. I'll call you Natushka, then. Little Natalie."

That didn't sound any more dignified but she decided not to argue.

When he left with the dog, she emptied the tote. The toothbrush came out of its protective plastic sleeve first. A good brushing made up for her earlier finger-work, but she grimaced when she tried to find a spot in the bathroom for the rest of her purchases.

The sink area was littered with shaving gear, a hairbrush with a few short hairs that might or might not belong to the dog, dental floss and a dusty bottle of aftershave with the cap crusted on. The rest of the bathroom wasn't much better. Her wrinkled clothes occupied the towel rack. A shampoo bottle lay tipped on its side in the shower. The damp towels from their morning showers were draped over the shower door.

When she swept her skirt, blouse and jacket from the rack, her nose wrinkled at the faint but still-present river smell. They were too far gone to salvage. Not that Natalie wanted to. She couldn't believe she'd traipsed around the capitals of Europe in such a shapeless, ugly suit. Wadding it into a ball, she took it to the kitchen and searched for a wastebasket.

She found one in the cupboard under the sink, right next to some basic cleaning supplies. The suit and blouse went in. A sponge, a bottle of glass cleaner and a spray can of foaming disinfectant came out. Since Dominic was letting her crash at his loft, the least she could do was clean up a little.

The bathroom was small enough that it didn't take her long to get it gleaming and smelling like an Alpine forest. On a roll, she attacked the kitchen next. The coffee mugs and breakfast plates hit the dishwasher. The paper napkins and white bag with its grease stains from the apple pancakes joined her clothes in the trash. The stovetop and oven door got a scrubbing, as did the dog dish in a corner next to a cupboard containing a giant-size bag of dried food. She opened the refrigerator, intending to wipe down the shelves, and jumped back.

"Omig…!"

Gulping, she identified the gory objects in the gallon-size plastic bag as bones. Big bones. Belonging, she guessed, to a cow or boar. The kind of bones a Hungarian hunting dog would gnaw to sharpen his teeth.

The only other objects in the fridge were a to-go carton from an Asian restaurant and a dozen or so bottles of beer with labels touting unfamiliar brands. Curiosity had her opening the cupboards above the sink and stove. She found a few staples, some spices and a half loaf of bread keeping company with a dusty bottle of something called

Tokaji. Dominic St. Sebastian, she decided, was not into cooking at home.

Abandoning the cupboards, she turned her attention to the stainless-steel sink. The scrubbing gave Natalie a sense of fierce satisfaction. She might not be a James Bond type but she knew how to take out sink and shower grunge!

The kitchen done, she attacked the sitting area. Books got straightened, old newspapers stacked. The sleek little laptop nested next to a pair of running shoes on the floor was moved to the drop-down shelf that doubled as a desk. Natalie ran her fingers over the keyboard, gripped by a sudden urge to power up the computer.

She was a research assistant, according to Dom. An archivist. She probably spent most of her waking hours on the computer. What would she find if she went online and researched one Natalie Clark? Or had Dom already done that? She'd have to ask him.

She was dusting the black-and-glass stand of the widescreen TV when he and the hound returned. The dog burst in first, of course, his claws tattooing on the oak floor. Dominic followed and placed a brown paper sack on the counter. Lifting a brow, he glanced at the now spotless kitchen.

"You've been busy."

"Just straightened up a bit. I hope you don't mind."

"Why would I mind?" Amusement glinted in his eyes. "Although I can think of better ways for both of us to work off excess energy than cleaning and dog walking."

She didn't doubt it for a moment. She was wearing proof of one of his workouts in the form of black silk hipsters. No doubt Kiss Kiss Arabella would supply an enthusiastic endorsement of his abilities in that area.

Not that Natalie required a second opinion. He'd already given her a hint of just how disturbing he could be to her equanimity if she let him. Which she wouldn't. She couldn't! Her life was in enough turmoil without adding the complication of a wild tumble between the sheets with Dominic St. Sebastian. The mere thought made her so nervous that she flapped the dust cloth like a shield.

"What's in the bag?"

"I stopped by the butcher shop and picked up our supper."

"I hope you've got more than bones in there," she said with a little grimace.

"You found those, did you?"

"They were hard to miss."

"Not to worry. Dog will take care of those, although I'm sure he would much rather share our goulash."

Natalie eyed the tall, round carton he extracted dubiously. "The butcher shop sells goulash?"

"No, but Frau Kemper, the butcher's wife, always makes extra for me when she cooks up a pot."

"Oh?" She caught the prune before it formed but couldn't quite keep the disdain from her tone. "It must be a burden having so many women showering you with gifts."

"It is," he said sadly. "A terrible burden. Especially Frau Kemper. If she keeps forcing stews and cakes on me, I'll soon match her weight of a hundred and fifty kilos or more."

"A hundred and fifty kilos?" Natalie did the math. "Ha! I'd like to see you at three hundred plus pounds."

"No, you would not." He cocked his head. "But you did that calculation very quickly."

"I did, didn't I?" Surprise gave way to panic. "How can I remember metric conversions and not my name? My past? Anything about my family?"

Dom hesitated a fraction of a second too long. He knew something. Something he didn't want to reveal.

"Tell me!" she said fiercely.

"Sarah says you have no family."

"What?" Her fist bunched, crumpling the cloth she'd forgotten she still held. "Everyone has family."

"Let me put the goulash on to simmer, and I'll tell you what I know. But first..." He reached into the bag again and produced a gold-labeled bottle. "I'll open this and we'll drink a glass while we talk, yes?"

A vague memory stirred. Something or someone splashing pale gold liquid into crystal snifter. A man? This man? Desperately, she fought to drag the details to the front of her mind.

"What's in the bottle?"

"A chardonnay from the Badacsony vineyards."

The fragments shifted, realigned, wouldn't fit together.

"Not...? Not apple brandy?"

"*Pálinka*? No," he said casually. Too casually. "That's what the duchess and I drank the last time I visited her in New York. You chose not to join us. This is much less potent."

He retrieved two wineglasses and rummaged in a drawer for an opener. She held up a hand before he poured. "None for me, thanks."

"Are you sure? It's light and crisp, one of Hungary's best whites."

"I'm not a drinker." As soon as the words were out, she sensed they were true. "You go ahead. I'm good with water."

"Then I'll have water, also."

With swift efficiency, he poured the goulash into a pot that had seen much better days. Once it was covered and set on low heat, he retrieved a bone for the hound and left him happily gnawing on the mat strategically placed under one of the eaves. Then he added ice to the two wineglasses and filled them with water.

"Let's take them to the balcony."

"Balcony," Natalie discovered when he held aside the

drapes on one side of the windows and opened an access door, was a grandiose term for the narrow platform that jutted out from the steep, sloping roof. Banded by a wrought-iron safety rail, it contained two bar chairs and a bistro-style table. Dominic edged past the table and settled in the farther chair.

Natalie had to drag in a deep breath before feeling her way cautiously to the closer chairs. She hitched up and peered nervously at the sheer drop on the other side of the railing.

"You're sure this is safe?"

"I'm sure. I built it myself."

Another persona. How many was that now? She had to do a mental recap. Grand Duke. Secret agent. Sex object of kissy-faced Englishwomen and full-bodied butcher's wives. General handyman and balcony-builder. All those facets to his personality, and hers was as flat and lifeless as a marble slab. More lifeless than she'd realized.

"You said I don't have any family," she prompted.

His glance strayed to the magnificence across the river. The slowly setting sun was gilding the turrets and spires and towering dome. The sight held him for several seconds. When it came back to her, Natalie braced herself.

"Sarah ran a background check on you before she hired you. According to her sources, there's no record of who your parents were or why they abandoned you as an infant. You were raised in a series of foster homes."

She must have known. On some subconscious level, she must have known. She'd been tossed out like trash. Unwanted. Unwelcome.

"You said a 'series' of foster homes. How many? Three? Five?"

"I don't have a number. I'll get one if you want."

"Never mind." Bitterness layered over the aching emptiness. "The total doesn't really matter, does it? What does is that in a country with couples desperate to adopt, apparently no one wanted me."

"You don't know that. I'm not familiar with adoption laws in the United States. There may have been some legal impediment."

He played with his glass, his long fingers turning the stem. There was more coming, and she guessed it wouldn't be good. It wasn't.

"We also have to take into account the fact that no one appears to have raised an alarm over your whereabouts. The Budapest police, my contacts at Interpol, Sarah and Dev…none of them have received queries or concerns that you may have gone missing."

"So in addition to no family, I have no friends or acquaintances close enough to worry about me."

She stared unseeing at the stunning vista of shining river and glittering spires. "What a pathetic life I must lead," she murmured.

"Perhaps."

She hadn't been fishing for a shoulder to cry on, but the less-than-sympathetic response rankled…until it occurred to her that he was holding something back.

The thought brought her head up with a snap. She scowled at him, sitting so calm and relaxed on his tiny handkerchief of a balcony. The slanting rays of the late-afternoon sun highlighted the short, glossy black hair, the golden oak of his skin, the strong cheekbones and chin. The speculative look in his dark eyes…

"What do you know that you're not telling me?" she snapped.

"There," he said, tipping his glass toward her in mock salute. "That's what I know."

"Huh?"

"That spark of temper. That flash of spirit. You try so

hard to hide them behind the prim, proper facade you present to the world but every so often they slip out."

"What are you talking about? What facade?"

He parried her questions with one of his own. "Do you see the ironmonger's cast there, right in front of you, stamped into the balcony railing?"

"What?"

"The cast mark. Do you see it?"

Frowning, she surveyed the ornate initial entwined with ivy. The mark was worn almost smooth but still legible. "You mean that *N*?"

He gestured with his glass again, this time at the panorama view across the river. "What about the Liberation Monument, high on that hill?

"Dominic…"

"Do you see it?"

She speared an impatient glance at the bronze statue of a woman holding a palm leaf high aloft. It dominated the hill in the far distance and could obviously be seen from anywhere in the city.

"Yes, I see it." The temper he'd commented on earlier sparked again. "But I'm in no mood for games or quizzes, Mr. Grand Duke. What do you know that I don't?"

"I know you wore glasses in New York," he replied evenly. "Large, square glasses with thick lenses that you apparently don't require for near or distance vision. I know you scraped your hair back most unattractively instead of letting it fall loose to your shoulders, as it does now. I know you chose loose clothes in an attempt to disguise your slender hips and—" his glance drifted south, and an appreciative gleam lit his eyes "—very delightful breasts."

Her mouth had started sagging at the mention of glasses. It dropped farther when he got to her hair, and snapped shut at the mention of her breasts. Fighting the urge to cross her arms over her chest, she tried to make sense of his observations.

She couldn't refute the part about the clothes. She'd questioned her fashion sense herself before she'd tossed the garments in the trash this morning. But the glasses? The hair?

She scrubbed her palms over her thighs, now encased in the formfitting designer jeans she'd purchased at the boutique. The jeans, the sandals, the short-sleeve T-shirt didn't feel strange or uncomfortable. From what Dom had said, though, they weren't her.

"Maybe what you saw in New York is the real me," she said a little desperately. "Maybe I just don't like drawing attention to myself."

"Maybe," he agreed, his gaze steady on her face. "And maybe there's a reason why you don't."

She could think of several reasons, none of them particularly palatable. Some were so far out she dismissed them instantly. She just couldn't see herself as a terrorist in training or a bank robber on the run. There was another explanation she couldn't shrug off as easily. One Dom brought up slowly, carefully.

"Perhaps your desire to hide the real you relates to a personal trauma, as Dr. Kovacs suggested this morning."

She couldn't deny the possibility. Yet...

She didn't *feel* traumatized. And she'd evidently been doing just fine before her dive into the Danube. She had a job that must have paid very well, judging by the advance on her salary Sarah had sent. She'd traveled to Paris, to Vienna, to Hungary. She must have an apartment back in the States. Books, maybe. Framed prints on the wall or a pen-and-ink sketch or a...

Her thoughts jerked to a stop. Rewound. Focused on a framed print. No, not a print. A painting. A canal scene with strong, hazy colors and a light so natural it looked as though the sun was shimmering on the water.

She could see it! Every sleek black gondola, every window arch framed by mellow stone, every ripple of the green waters of the lagoon.

"Didn't Sarah tell you I went to Vienna to research a painting?" she asked Dom eagerly.

"She did."

"A Venetian canal scene." She clung to the mental image with a fierce effort of will. "By...by..."

"Canaletto."

"Yes!" She edged off the tall chair and kept a few careful inches away from the iron railing. "Let's go inside. I need to use your laptop."

Seven

The spicy scent of paprika and simmering beef filled the loft when they went inside. Natalie sniffed appreciatively but cut a straight line for the laptop.

"Do I need a password to power up?"

"Just hit the on switch."

"Really?" She dropped into the leather armchair and positioned the laptop on her knees. "I would have thought 007 would employ tighter security."

Dom didn't bother to explain that all electronic and digital communications he received from or sent to Interpol were embedded with so many layers of encryption that no one outside the agency could decipher them. He doubted she would have heard him in any case. She was hunched forward, her fingers hovering over the keys.

"I hope you have Wi-Fi," she muttered as the screen brightened to display a close-up of the hound. All nose and bright eyes and floppy ears, the image won a smile from Natalie. The real thing plopped down on his haunches before Dom and let his tongue loll in eager anticipation of a libation.

Idly, Dom tipped some lager into his dish and watched as Natalie skimmed through site after site relating to the eighteenth-century Italian painter. The cop in him kept returning to their conversation outside on the balcony. He wasn't buying her quick dismissal of the suggestion she'd tried to downplay her natural beauty.

She most definitely had, and the ploy hadn't worked. Not with Dom, anyway. Despite her disdainful sniffs, daunting glasses and maiden-aunt clothes, she'd stirred his interest from the moment she'd opened the door of the duchess's apartment. And she'd damned near tied him in knots when she'd paraded out of the shower this morning with that crew shirt skimming her thighs.

Now...

His fist tightened on the dew-streaked pilsner bottle. She should see herself through his eyes. The shoulder-length, honey-streaked brown hair. The fierce concentration drawing her brows into a straight line. The lips pooched into a tight rosebud.

Jézus, Mária és József! Those lips!

Swallowing a groan, Dom took another pull of the lager and gave the rest to the ecstatic hound.

"You shouldn't let him have beer."

He glanced over to find her looking all prudish and disapproving again. Maybe it wasn't a disguise, he thought wryly. Maybe there was room in that sexy body for a nun, a shower scrubber and a wanton.

God, he hoped so!

It didn't take her long to find what she was looking for. Dom was still visualizing a steamy shower encounter when she whooped.

"This is it! This is the painting I was researching. I don't know how I know it, but I do."

He crossed the room and peered over her shoulder. Her scent drifted up to him, mingling with that of the goulash to tease his senses. Hair warmed by the sun. Skin dusted from their day in the city. The faint tang of cleaning solutions. Excitement radiated from her as she read him the details she'd pulled up on the laptop.

"It's one of Canaletto's early works. Commissioned by a Venetian doge and seized by Napoleon as part of the spoils of war after he invaded Venice in 1797. It reportedly hung in his study at the Tuileries Palace, then disappeared sometime before or during a fire in 1871."

She scrolled down the page. She was in full research mode now, inhaling every detail with the same eagerness the hound did pilsner.

"The painting disappeared for almost a half a century, until it turned up again in the early '30s in the private collection of a Swiss industrialist. He died in 1953 and his squabbling heirs auctioned off his entire collection. At that point... Look!"

She stabbed a finger at the screen. Dom bent closer.

"At that point," she recited eagerly, "it was purchased by an agent acting for the Grand Duke of Karlenburgh."

She swiveled around, almost tilting the laptop off her knees in her eagerness. Her face was alive, her eyes bright with the thrill of discovery.

"The Grand Duke of Karlenburgh," she repeated. "That was you, several times removed."

"*Many* times removed."

Despite his seeming insouciance, the connection couldn't be denied. It wove around him like a fine, silken thread. Trapping him. Cocooning him.

"The painting was a gift from the duke to his duchess," he related, remembering the mischievous look in Charlotte's eyes. "To commemorate a particularly pleasant visit to Venice."

Natalie's face went blank for a moment, then lit with excitement. "I remember hearing that story! Venice is where she got pregnant, right? With her only child?"

"Right."

They were so close, her mouth just a breath away from

his, that Dom couldn't help himself. He had to drop a kiss on those tantalizing lips.

He kept it light, playful. But when he raised his head confusion and a hint of wariness had replaced the excitement. Kicking himself, he tried to coax it back.

"Charlotte said the painting hung in the Red Salon at Karlenburgh Castle. Is there reference to that?"

"I, uh… Let me look."

She ducked her head and hit the keys again. Her hair feathered against her cheek like a sparrow's wing, shielding her face. He knew he'd lost serious ground when she shook her head and refused to look at him.

"No mention here. All it says is that the painting was lost again in the chaos following the Soviet suppression of the 1956 Hungarian Uprising."

"The same uprising that cost the Grand Duke his life and forced his wife to flee her homeland."

"How sad." With a small sigh, Natalie slumped against the chair back. "Charlotte's husband purchased the painting to celebrate one of the most joyous moments of their lives. And just a little more than a year later, both he and the painting were lost."

Her voice had gone small and quiet. She was drawing parallels, Dom guessed. Empathizing with the duchess's tragic losses. Feeling the emptiness of her own life.

The thought of her being a forgotten, helpless cog in a vast social welfare bureaucracy pulled at something deep inside him. He'd known her for such a short time. Had spoken to her twice in New York. Spent less than twenty-four hours with her here in Budapest. Yet he found himself wanting to erase the empty spaces in her heart. To pull her into his arms and fill the gaps in her mind with new, happy and extremely erotic memories. The urge was so powerful it yanked him up like a puppet on a twisted string.

Christ! He was a cop. Like all cops, he knew that trust

could—and too often did—shift like the sand on a wave-swept shore. Identities had to be validated, backgrounds scrubbed with a wire brush. Until he heard back from his contact at Interpol, he'd damned well better keep his hands to himself.

"The duke was executed," he said briskly, "but Charlotte survived. She made a new life for herself and her baby in New York. Now she has her granddaughters, her great-grandchildren. And you, Ms. Clark, have the finest goulash in all of Budapest to sample."

The abrupt change in direction accomplished precisely what he'd intended. Natalie raised her head. The curtain of soft, shiny hair fell back, and a tentative smile etched across her face.

"I'm ready."

More than ready, she realized. They hadn't eaten since their hurried breakfast and it was now almost seven. The aroma filling the loft had her taste buds dancing in eagerness.

"Ha!" Dom said with a grin. "You may think you're prepared, but Frau Kemper's stew is in a class by itself. Prepare for a culinary tsunami."

While he sniffed and stirred the goulash, Natalie set the counter with the mismatched crockery and cutlery she'd found during her earlier explorations of the kitchen cupboards.

Doing the homey little task made her feel strange. Strange and confused and nervous. Especially when her hip bumped Dominic's in the narrow kitchen area. And when he reached for a paper towel the same time she did. And...

Oh, for pity's sake! Who was she kidding? It wasn't the act of laying out bowls and spoons that had her mind and nerves jumping. It was Dominic. She couldn't look at him without remembering the feel of his mouth on hers.

Couldn't listen to him warning the dog—Duke!—to take himself out of the kitchen without thinking about how he'd called her sweetheart in Hungarian. And not just in Hungarian. In a husky, teasing voice that seemed so intimate, so seductive.

She didn't really know him. Hell, she didn't even know herself! Yet when he went to refill her glass with water she stopped him.

"I'd like to try that wine you brought home."

He looked up from the spigot in surprise. "Are you sure?"

"Yes."

She was. She really was. Natalie had no idea what lay at the root of her aversion to alcohol. A secretive, guilt-ridden tasting as a kid? An ugly drunk as a teen? A degrading experience in college? Whatever had caused it remained shrouded in her past. Right here, though, right now, she felt safe enough enjoy a glass of wine.

Safe?

The word echoed in her mind as Dom worked the cork on the chilled bottle and raised his glass to eye level. *"Egészségére!"*

"I'll drink to that, whatever it means."

"It means 'to your health.' Unless you mispronounce it," he added with a waggle of his brows. "Then it means 'to your arse.'"

She didn't bother to ask which pronunciation he'd used, just took a sip and waited for some unseen ax to fall. When the cool, refreshing white went down smoothly, she started to relax.

The goulash sped that process considerably. The first spoonful had her gasping and reaching desperately for the wineglass. The second, more cautious spoonful went down with less of an assault by the paprika and garlic. By the third, she'd recovered enough to appreciate the subtle flavors of caraway seed, marjoram and sautéed onions. By the fourth, she was spearing the beef, pork and potatoes with avid enthusiasm and sopping up gravy with chunks of dark bread torn from the loaf Frau Kemper had thoughtfully included with her stew.

She limited her wine intake to a single glass but readily agreed to a second helping of goulash. The Agár sat on his haunches beside her stool as she spooned it down. When she didn't share, his liquid brown eyes filled with such reproach that she was forced to sneak him several dripping morsels. Dom pretended not to notice, although he did mention drily that he'd have to take the hound for an extralong run before bed to flush the spicy stew out of his system.

As casual as it was, the comment started Natalie's nerves jumping again. The loft boasted only one bed. She'd occupied it last night. She felt guilty claiming it again.

"Speaking of bed…"

Dom's spoon paused in midair. "Yes?"

Her cheeks heating, she stirred the last of her stew. He had to be wondering why she hadn't taken Sarah up on her offer of a hotel room. At the moment, she couldn't help wondering the same thing.

"I don't like ousting you out of yours."

"Oh?" His spoon lowered. "Are you suggesting we share?"

She was becoming familiar with that slow, provocative grin.

"I'm suggesting," she said with a disdainful sniff, "I sleep on the sofa tonight and you take the bed."

She hadn't intended her retort as a challenge, but she should have known Dom would view it that way. Laughter leaped into his face, along with something that started Natalie's breath humming in her throat.

"Ah, sweetheart," he murmured, his eyes on her mouth.

"You make it very difficult for me to ignore the instincts bred into me by my wild, marauding ancestors."

Even Duke seemed to sense the sudden tension that arced through her. The dog wedged closer to Natalie and propped his head on her knee. She knuckled his forehead and tried desperately to blank any and all thought of Dom tossing her over his shoulder. Carrying her to his bed. Pillaging her mouth. Ravishing her body. Demanding a surrender she was all too willing to...

"Don't look so worried."

The wry command jolted her back to the here and now. Blinking, she watched Dom push off his stool.

"My blood may run as hot as my ancestors', but I draw the line at seducing a woman who can't remember her name. Come, Dog."

Still racked by the erotic images, Natalie bent her head to avoid looking at Dom as he snapped the Agár's lead to his collar. She couldn't avoid the knuckle he curved under her chin, however, or the real regret in his eyes when he tipped her face to his.

"I'm sorry, Natushka. I shouldn't tease you. I know this is a frightening time for you."

Oh, sure. Like she was going to tell him that fright was *not* what she was feeling right now? Easing her chin from his hold, she slid off her stool and gathered the used utensils.

"I'll wash the dishes while you're gone."

"No need. Just stick them in the dishwasher."

"Go!" She needed to do something with her hands and her overactive, overheated mind. "I'll take care of the kitchen."

She did the dishes. Spritzed the sink and countertop. Drew the drapes. Fussed with paperbacks she'd stacked earlier that afternoon. Curled up in the chair and reached for the laptop. And grew more annoyed with each passing moment.

Her glance kept darting from the wide sofa with its worn leather cushions to the bed tucked under the eaves at the far end of the loft. She didn't understand why she was so irritated by Dom's assurance that he wouldn't seduce her. Those brief moments of fantasy involving marauding Magyars aside, she didn't really *want* him to. Did she?

Lips compressed, she tried to balance her contradictory emotions. On the one hand, Dominic St. Sebastian constituted the only island in the empty sea of her mind. It was natural that she would cling to him. Not want to antagonize him or turn him away.

Yet what she was feeling now wasn't mental. It was physical, and growing more urgent by the moment. She wanted his hands on her, dammit! His mouth. She wanted that hard, muscled body pinning hers to the wall, the sheets, even the floor.

The intensity of the hunger pumping through her veins surprised her. It also generated an enormous relief. All that talk about a possible past trauma had raised some ugly questions in her mind. In Dom's, too, apparently, judging by his comment about her deliberately trying to downplay her looks. The realization that she could want a man as much as she appeared to want this one was as reassuring as it was frustrating.

Which brought her right back to square one. She threw another thoroughly annoyed look at the bed. She should have taken Sarah up on her offer to arrange a hotel room, she thought sourly. If she had, she wouldn't be sitting here wondering whether she should—or could!—convince Dom to forget about being all noble and considerate.

Shoving out of the chair, she stalked to the wardrobe and reclaimed the shirt she'd slept in last night. She took it into the bathroom to change, and her prickly irritation ratcheted up another notch when she found the hand towel she'd left folded neatly over the rack tossed in a damp pile atop the counter. Worse, the toiletries she'd carefully arranged to make room for her few purchases were once again scattered haphazardly around the sink.

Muttering, she stripped off her new jeans and top. She didn't think she was obsessive-compulsive. And even if she was, what was so wrong with keeping things neat and orderly?

The sight of her borrowed undies didn't exactly improve her mood. Dom obviously hadn't suffered from an excess of scruples with Kissy Face Arabella. Natalie would have dumped the black silk hipsters in the trash if she'd had another pair to step into. She'd have to do more shopping tomorrow.

Yanking the crew shirt over her head, she scrubbed her face and teeth. Then she carefully refolded *her* towel and scooped up her jeans and top. Just as she exited the bathroom, the front door opened and Duke bounded in. His ecstatic greeting soon had her laughing. Hard to stay in a snit with a cold nose poking her bare thighs and a pink tongue determined to slather her with kisses.

"Okay, enough, stop." She fended off a determined lunge and pointed a stern finger at the floor. "Duke! Sit!"

He looked a little confused by the English command but the gesture got through to him. Ears flopping, he dropped onto his haunches.

"Good boy." She couldn't resist sending his master a smug look. "See, he recognizes his name."

"I think he recognized your tone."

"Whatever." She chewed on her lower lip for a moment. "We didn't resolve the issue of the bed earlier. I don't feel right consigning you to the sofa. I'll sleep there tonight."

"No, you won't."

"Look, I'm very grateful for all you've done for me. I

don't want to inconvenience you any more than I already have."

Dom managed not to snort. If she had any idea of just how badly she was "inconveniencing" him at this moment, she'd shimmy back into her jeans and run like hell. Instead she just stood there while his gaze gobbled up the long, slender legs showing below the hem of his shirt. The mere thought of those legs tangled with his started an ache in his groin.

He damned well better not fantasize about what was *under* the shirt. If he did, neither one of them would make it to the bed. They might not even make it to the sofa.

"I've fallen asleep more nights than I can count in front of the TV," he bit out. "You've got the bed."

He could tell from the way her mouth set that he'd come across more brusque than he'd intended. Tough. After just a little more than twenty-four hours in her company, Ms. Clark had him swinging like a pendulum. One moment his cop's instincts were reminding him that things weren't always what they seemed. The next, he ached to take her in his arms and kiss away the fear she was doing her best to disguise.

Now he just plain ached, and he wasn't happy about the fact that he couldn't—wouldn't!—do anything to ease the hurt. And why was she tormenting him like this, anyway?

"You're not going to bed now, are you?" he asked her.

"It's almost ten."

He managed to keep his jaw from sagging, but it took a heroic effort. He could understand her crashing facedown on the bed last night. She'd been hurt. She'd spent who knew how long in the Danube, and had a lump the size of a softball at the base of the skull.

She'd seemed to recover today, though. Enough for him to make an incautious comment. "At ten o'clock most Hungarians are trying to decide where to go for coffee and dessert."

Her chin tilted. "If you want to go out for coffee and dessert, please don't let me stop you."

Whoa! He'd missed something here. When he left to take out the dog twenty minutes ago, Natalie had been all soft and shy and confused. Now she was as stiff and prickly as a horsehair blanket.

Dom wanted to ask what happened in that short time span but he'd learned the hard way to keep his mouth shut. He'd guided his sister through her hormone-driven teen years. He'd also enjoyed the company of his fair share of women. Enough, anyway, to know that any male who attempted to plumb the workings of the female mind had better be wearing a Kevlar vest. Since he wasn't, he quickly backpedaled.

"Probably just as well we make it an early night. We have a full day tomorrow."

She acknowledged his craven retreat with a regal dip of her head. "Yes, we do. Good night."

"Good night."

Dom and the hound both watched as she made her way to the far end of the loft and arranged her jeans and tank top into neat folds before placing them on the table beside the bed. Dom didn't move while she turned back the comforter and slid between the sheets.

The dog didn't exercise the same restraint. His claws scrabbling on the oak floorboards, he scrambled across the open space and made a flying leap. He landed on the bed with paws outstretched and announced his arrival with a happy woof. Natalie laughed and eased to one side to make room for him.

With a muttered curse, Dom turned away from the sight of the Agár sprawled belly-up beside her.

Eight

The next day dawned achingly bright and gloriously cool. The first nip of fall had swept away the exhaust-polluted city air and left Budapest sparkling in the morning light.

Dom woke early after a restless night. Natalie was still hunched under the featherbed when he took the hound for his morning run. Halfway through their usual five miles he received a text message with a copy of her driver's license. He saved the attachment to print out at the loft and thumbed his phone to access the US Embassy website. Once he'd downloaded the application to replace a lost passport, he made a note to himself to call the consular office and set up an appointment.

He was tempted to make another call to his contact at Interpol. When he'd asked Andre to dig deeper, he hadn't expected the excavation to take more than a day. Two at the most. But he knew Andre would get back to him if he uncovered anything of interest.

Dom also knew he belonged in the field! He'd taken down vicious killers, drug traffickers, the remorseless sleaze who sold children to the highest bidders. He didn't claim to be the best at what he did, but he'd done his part. This extended vacation was pure crap.

Or had been, until Natalie had dropped into his life. If Dom hadn't been at such loose ends he might not have been so quick to assume complete responsibility for her.

Now that he had, he felt obligated to keep her close until her memory returned.

It was already trickling back. Bits and pieces had started to pierce the haze. And when the fog dissipated completely, he thought with a sudden tightening of his belly, he intended to do his damnedest to follow up on that one, searing kiss. He'd spent too many uncomfortable hours on the sofa last night, imagining just that eventuality.

A jerk on the leash checked his easy stride. He glanced down to see the hound dragging his rear legs and glaring at him reproachfully.

"Don't look at me like that. You're already in bed with her."

Still the dog wouldn't move.

"Oh, all right. Have at it."

Dom jogged in place while the Agár sniffed the interesting pile just off the track, then majestically lifted a leg to spray it.

As soon as Dom and the hound entered, they were hit with the aroma of sizzling bacon and freshly baked cinnamon bread. The scents were almost as tantalizing as the sight of Natalie at the stove, a spatula in hand and a towel tucked apronlike around her slim hips. Dom tried to remember the last woman who'd made herself at home in his kitchen. None of those who'd come for a drink and stayed for the night, as best he could recall. And certainly not his sister. Even as a child, Anastazia had always been too busy splinting the broken wings of sparrows or feeding baby squirrels with eyedroppers to think about nourishing herself or her brother.

"I went down to the grocery shop on the corner," Natalie said by way of greeting. "I thought we should have breakfast before we took off for Karlenburgh Castle."

"That sounds good. How long before it's ready?"

"Five minutes."

"Make it ten," he begged.

He snagged a cup of coffee and had to hide a grimace. She'd made it American style. Closer to colored water than the real thing. The weak brew provided barely enough punch to get him through a quick shower and shave.

He emerged eager for a taste of the bacon laid out in crisp strips on a paper towel. The fluffy eggs scrambled with mushrooms and topped with fresh-grated Gruyère cheese had his tongue hanging out almost as far as the hound's. But the warm cinnamon rolls tucked in a napkin made him go weak at the knees. Groaning, he sank onto a stool at the counter.

"Do you cook breakfast for yourself every morning?"

She paused with the spatula hovering above the platter of eggs. "I don't know."

"No matter," Dom said fervently. "You're doing fine."

Actually, she was doing great. Her movements concise and confident, she set out his mismatched plates and folded paper napkins into neat, dainty triangles. Amused, he saw that she'd purchased a small bouquet of flowers during her quick trip to the grocers. The purple lupines and pink roses now sprouted from his prized beer stein. He had to admit they added a nice touch of color to the otherwise drab kitchen area.

So did she. She wore the jeans she'd purchased yesterday and had borrowed another of his soccer shirts. The hem of the hunter-green shirt fell well below her hips, unfortunately, but when she leaned across the counter to refill his coffee mug, the deep-V neckline gave him a tantalizing glimpse of creamy slopes.

Promising the hopeful hound he would be fed later, she perched on the stool beside Dom and served them both. The eggs tasted as good as they looked. He was halfway through his when he gave her an update.

"While I was out jogging, I got a text with a copy of your driver's license attached. I also downloaded the application form for a replacement passport. I'll print both after breakfast, then we'll make an appointment with the consular office."

Natalie nodded. The bits and pieces of her life seemed to be falling into place. She just wished they would fall faster. Maybe this excursion to Karlenburgh Castle would help. Suddenly impatient, she hopped off her stool and rinsed her dish in the sink.

"Are you finished?" she asked.

He relinquished his plate but snagged the last cinnamon bun before she could whisk the basket away. She did a quick kitchen cleanup and changed back into her red tank top. Her straw tote hooked over her shoulder, she waited impatiently while Dom extracted a lightweight jacket from his wardrobe.

"You'll need this. It can get cool up in the mountains."

She was disappointed when he decreed the hound wouldn't join them on the expedition…and surprised when he introduced her to the girl in the apartment downstairs who looked after the animal during his frequent absences.

The dog-sitter wasn't the sultry, predatory single Natalie had imagined. Instead she looked to be about nine or ten, with a splash of freckles across her nose and a backpack that indicated she'd been just about to depart for school.

When she dropped to her knees to return the hound's eager kisses, her papa came to the door. Dom introduced Natalie and explained that they might return late. "I would appreciate it if Katya would walk him after school, as per our usual agreement."

The father smiled fondly at his daughter and replied in heavily accented English. "But of course, Dominic. They will both enjoy the exercise. We still have the bones and bag of food you left last time. If you are late, we'll feed him, yes?"

"We should not call him Dominic anymore, Papa." The girl sent Dom an impish grin. "We should address you as Your Grace, shouldn't we?"

"You do," he retorted, tugging on her ear, "and I won't let you download any more songs from my iTunes account."

Giggling, she pulled away and reminded him of a promise he looked as though he would prefer to forget. "You're coming to my school, aren't you? I want to show off my important neighbor."

"Yes, yes. I will."

"When?"

"Soon."

"When?"

"Katya," her father said in gentle reproof.

"But Dom's on vacation now. He told us so." Her arm looped around the dog's neck, she turned accusing eyes on her upstairs neighbor. "So when will you come?"

Natalie had to bite the inside of her lip to keep from laughing. The kid had him nailed and knew it.

"Next week," he promised reluctantly.

"When next week?"

"Katya, enough!"

"But, Papa, I need to tell my teacher when to expect the Grand Duke of Karlenburgh."

Groaning, Dom committed to Tuesday afternoon if her teacher concurred. Then he grasped Natalie's elbow and steered her toward the garage stairs.

"Let's get out of here before she makes me promise to wear a crown and a purple robe."

"Yes, Your Grace."

"Watch yourself, woman."

"Yes, Your Grace."

She knew him well enough now to laugh off his bad-tempered growl. As they started down the winding streets of Castle Hill, though, she added another facet to his growing list of alter egos. Undercover Agent. Grand Duke. Rescuer of damsels in distress. Loving older brother. Adopter of stray hounds. And now friend to an obviously adoring preteen.

Then there was that other side to him. The hot, sexy marauder whose ancestors had swept down from the Steppes. Sitting right next to her, so close that all she had to do was slide a glance at his profile to remember his taste and his scent and the feel of all those hard muscles pressed against her.

Natalie bit her lip in dismay when she realized she couldn't decide which of Dom's multiple personalities appealed to her most. They were all equally seductive, and she had the scary feeling that she was falling a little bit in love with each one of them.

Lost in those disturbing thoughts, she didn't see they'd emerged onto a broad boulevard running parallel to the Danube until Dom pointed out an impressive complex with an elaborate facade boasting turrets and fanciful wrought-iron balconies.

"That's Gellért Hotel. Their baths are among the best in Budapest. We'll have to follow Dr. Kovacs's advice and go for a soak tomorrow, yes?"

Natalie couldn't remember if she'd been to a communal bath before. Somehow it didn't seem like her kind of thing. "Do the spa-goers wear bathing suits?"

"In the public pools." He tipped her a quick grin. "But we can book a private session, where suits are optional."

Like that was going to happen! Natalie could barely breathe sitting here next to him fully clothed. She refused to think about the two of them slithering into a pool naked.

Hastily, she shoved her thoughts in a different direction. "How far did you say it was to where I left the rental car?"

"Győr's only a little over a hundred kilometers."

"And Pradzéc, where I crossed over from Austria?"

"Another sixty or seventy kilometers. But the going will be slower as we get closer to the border. The road winds as it climbs into the Alps."

"Where it reaches Karlenburgh Castle," she murmured.

She'd been there. She *knew* she'd been there. Dom claimed the castle was nothing but a pile of tumbled rock now but something had pulled Natalie to those ruins. Even now, she could feel the tug. The sensation was so strong, so compelling, that it took her some time to let go of it and pay more attention to the countryside they passed through.

They zipped along the M1 motorway as it cut through the region that Dom told her was called Northern Transdanubia. Despite its bloody history as the traditional battleground between Hungary and the forces invading from the west, the region was one of gentle hills, green valleys and lush forests. The international brown signs designating a significant historic landmark flashed by with astonishing frequency. Each town or village they passed seemed to boast an ancient abbey or spa or fortified stronghold.

The city of Győr was no exception. When Dom pointed out that it was located exactly halfway between Vienna and Budapest, she wondered how many armies had tramped through its ancient, cobbled streets. Natalie caught only a glimpse of Old Town's battlements, however, before they turned north. Short moments later they reached the point where two smaller rivers flowed into the mighty Danube.

A double-decker tour boat was just departing the wharf. Natalie strained every brain cell in an effort to identify with the day-trippers crowding the rails on the upper decks. Nothing clicked. Not even when Dom turned into the parking lot and parked next to the motorized matchbox she'd supposedly rented in Vienna almost two days ago.

Dom had arranged for a rental agency rep to meet them. When the agent popped the trunk with a spare set of keys a tingle began to feather along her nerves. The tingle surged to a hot, excited rush the moment she spotted a bulging leather briefcase.

"That's mine!"

Snatching the case out of the trunk, she cradled it against her breasts like a long-lost baby. She allowed it out of her arms only long enough for Dom to note the initials embossed in gold near the handle...and the fact that it wasn't locked. Her heart pounding, she popped the latch and whooped at the sight of a slim laptop jammed between stacks of fat files.

"This must be yours, too," the rental agency rep said as he lifted out a weekender on wheels.

She didn't experience the same hot rush when the ID tag on the case verified the case was, in fact, hers. Maybe because when she opened it to inspect the contents they looked as though they belonged to an octogenarian. Everything was drab, colorless and eminently sensible. She tried to pump herself up with the realization that she now had several sets of clean undies in her possession. Unfortunately, they were all plain, unadorned undies that Kiss Kiss Arabella wouldn't be caught dead in!

A check of the vehicle's interior produced no purse, passport, ID or credit cards. Nor was there any sign of the glasses Dominic insisted she hadn't really needed. They must have gone into the river with her. Hugging the briefcase, she watched as Dom transferred the weekender to his own car and provided a copy of the police report to the rep from the rental agency. In view of her accident and injury and the fact that there was no apparent damage to the vehicle, the rep agreed to waive the late return charges.

Natalie almost shivered with impatience to delve into the files in the briefcase but Dom wanted to talk to the people at the tour office first on the off-chance they might remember her. They didn't, nor could they provide any more information than the police had already gleaned by tracking her credit card charges.

Natalie stood with Dom next to the ticket booth and stared at the sleek boat now little more than a speck in the distance. "This is so frustrating! Why did I take a river cruise? I don't even like boats."

"How do you know?"

She blinked. "I'm not sure. I just don't."

"Maybe we'll find a clue in your briefcase."

She glanced around the wharf area, itching to get into those fat files, but knew they couldn't spread their contents out on a picnic table where the breeze off the river might snatch them away. Dom sensed her frustration and offered a suggestion.

"We're less than an hour from Karlenburgh Castle. There's an inn in the village below the castle ruins. We can have lunch and ask Frau Dortmann for the use of her parlor to lay everything out."

"Let's go!"

She couldn't resist extracting a few of the files and skimming through them on the way. Each folder was devoted to a lost treasure. A neat table of contents listed everything inside—printed articles from various computer sources, copies of handwritten documents, color photos, black-and-whites, historical chronologies tracing last known ownership, notes Natalie had made to herself on additional sources to check.

"Ooh," she murmured when she flipped to a sketch of jewel-studded egg nested in a gold chariot pulled by a winged cherub. "How beautiful."

Dom glanced at the photo. "Isn't that the Fabergé egg Tsar Alexander gave his wife?"

"I...uh..." She checked her notes and looked up in surprise. "It is. How do you know that?"

"You were researching it in the States. You told me about it when we got together in your hotel room in New York."

"We got together in New York? In my hotel room?"

Dom was tempted, really tempted, but he stuck with the truth. "I thought you might be scheming to rip off the duchess with all that business about the codicil so I came to warn you off. You," he added with a quick grin, "kicked me out on my ass."

The Natalie he knew and was beginning to seriously lust after emerged. "I'm sure you deserved it."

"Ah, Natushka. Don't go all prim and proper on me. We might not make it to the inn."

He said it with a smile but they both knew he was only half kidding. Cheeks flushed, Natalie dug into the file again.

She saw the castle ruins first. She could hardly miss them. The tumbled walls and skeletal remains of a single square tower were set high on a rocky crag and visible from miles away. As they got closer, Natalie could see how the road cut through the narrow pass below—the only pass connecting Austria and Hungary for fifty miles in either direction, Dom informed her.

"No wonder the Habsburgs were so anxious to have your ancestors hold it for the Empire."

Only after they'd topped a steep rise did she see the village at the base of the cliffs. The dozen or so structures were typically Alpine, half-timbered and steep-roofed to slough off snow. A wooden roadside shrine housing a statue of the Virgin Mary greeted them as they approached the village. In keeping with the mingled heritage of the residents, the few street signs and notices were in both German and Hungarian.

The gasthaus sat at the edge of the village. Its mossy shingles and weathered timbers suggested it had welcomed wayfarers for centuries. Geraniums bloomed in every window box and an ivy-covered beer garden beckoned at one side of the main structure.

When Natalie and Dom went up the steps and entered the knotty-pine lobby, the woman who hustled out to greet them didn't match her rustic surroundings. Dom's casual reference to Frau Dortmann had evoked hazy images of an apron-clad, rosy-cheeked matron.

The fortysomething blonde in leggings and a tiger-striped tunic was as far from matronly as a woman could get. And if there was a Herr Dortmann hanging around anywhere, Natalie was certain he wouldn't appreciate the way his wife flung herself into Dom's arms. Wrapping herself around him like a half-starved boa constrictor, she kissed him. Not on both cheeks like any other polite European, but long and hard and full on the lips.

He was half laughing, half embarrassed when he finally managed to extricate himself. With a rueful glance at Natalie, he interrupted the blonde's spate of rapid Hungarian liberally interspersed with German.

"Lisel, this is Natalie Clark. A friend of mine from America."

"America!" Wide, amethyst eyes turned to Natalie. Eager hands reached out to take both of hers. "*Wilkommen!* You must come in. You'll have a lager, *ja*? And then you will tell me how you come to be in the company of a rogue such as Dominic St. Sebastian." Her laughing glance cut back to Dom. "Or do I address you as 'Your Grace'? *Ja, ja,* I must. The whole village talks of nothing else but the stories about you in the papers."

"You can thank Natalie for that," he drawled.

The blonde's brows soared. "How so?"

"She's an archivist. A researcher who digs around in musty old ledgers. She uncovered a document in Vienna that appears to grant the titles of Grand Duke and Duchess of Karlenburgh to the St. Sebastians until the Alps crumble. As we all know, however, it's an empty honor."

"Ha! Not here. As soon as word gets around that the Grand Duke has returned to his ancestral home, the taproom will be jammed and the beer will flow like a river. Just wait. You will see."

They didn't have to wait long. Dom had barely finished explaining to Frau Dortman that he'd only come to show Natalie the ruins and aid her in her research when the door opened. A bent, craggy-faced gentleman in worn leather pants hobbled in and greeted Dom with the immense dignity of a man who'd lived through good times and bad. This, Natalie soon grasped, was a good time. A very good time, the older man indicated with a wide smile.

He was followed in short order by a big, buff farmer who carried the sharp tang of the barn in with him, two teenagers with curious eyes and earbuds dangling around their necks and a young woman cradling a baby on her hip. Natalie kept waiting for Herr Dortmann to make an appearance. When he didn't show, a casual query revealed Lisel had divorced the lazy good-for-nothing and sent him packing years ago.

Dom tried his best to include Natalie in the conversations that buzzed around them. As more and more people arrived, though, she edged out of the inner circle and enjoyed the show. St. Sebastian might downplay this whole royalty thing, she mused as she settled on a bar stool and placed her briefcase on a counter worn smooth by centuries of use, but he was a natural. It wasn't so much that he stood two or three inches above the rest of the crowd. Or that he exuded such an easy self-confidence. Or, she thought wryly, that he had already informed Lisel that he would pay for the beer that flowed as freely as the innkeeper had predicted.

He also, Natalie guessed, paid for the platters piled with sausages and spaetzle and fried potatoes and pickled beets that emerged in successive waves from the kitchen. The feasting and toasts and storytelling lasted through the afternoon and into the evening. By then, Dom had downed too much beer to get behind the wheel again.

Lisel had anticipated just such an eventuality. "You will stay here tonight," she announced and drew an old-fashioned iron key from the pocket of her tiger-striped tunic. "The front bedroom has a fine view of the castle," she confided to Natalie. "You and Dominic can see it as you lie in bed."

"It sounds wonderful." She plucked the room key out of the innkeeper's hand. "But Dominic will need other sleeping arrangements."

After Lisel Dortmann's enthusiastic welcome, Natalie preferred not to speculate on what those arrangements might be. All she knew was that she wasn't going to share a bed with the man—as much as she wanted to.

Nine

She took the narrow wooden stairs to the second floor and found the front bedroom easily enough. It contained a good-size bath and an alcove tucked under the slanting eaves that housed a small desk and overstuffed easy chair. The beautifully carved wooden headboard and washstand with its porcelain pitcher and bowl provided antique touches, while the flat-screen TV and small placard announcing the inn offered free Wi-Fi were welcome modern conveniences.

As Lisel had promised, the lace-draped windows offered an unimpeded view of the ruins set high atop the rocky promontory. The early evening shadows lent them a dark and brooding aspect. Then the clouds shifted, parted, and the last of the sun's rays cut like a laser. For a few magical moments what remained of Karlenburgh Castle was bathed in bright gold.

She'd seen these ruins before! Natalie knew it! Not all shimmery and ethereal and golden like this but...

A rap on the door interrupted her tumultuous thoughts. Dom stood in the hall with the weekender he'd brought in from the car.

"I thought you might need your case."

"Thanks." She grabbed his arm and hauled him toward the window. "You've got to see this."

He glanced through the windows at the sight she pointed

to but almost immediately his gaze switched back to Natalie. Her eyes were huge, her face alive with excitement. She could hardly contain it as she turned to him.

"Those ruins… That setting… I went up there, Dom."

Her forehead scrunched with such an intense effort to dredge up stubborn memories that it hurt him to watch. Aching for her, he raised his hand and traced his thumb down the deep crease in her brow. He followed the slope of her nose, the line of her tightly folded lips.

"Ah, Natushka." The husky murmur distracted her, as he'd intended. "You're doing it again."

"Doing wh…? Oh."

He couldn't help himself. He had to coax those lips back to lush, ripe fullness. Then, of course, he had to take his fill of them. To his delight, she tilted her head to give him better access.

He wasn't sure when he knew a mere taste wouldn't be enough. Maybe when she gave a little sigh and leaned into him. Or when her hands slid up and over his shoulders. Or when the ache he'd felt when he'd watched her struggling to remember dropped south. Hard and heavy and suddenly hurting, he tried to disentangle.

"No!"

The command was breathy and urgent. She tightened her arms around his neck, dragging him in for another kiss. This time she gave, and Dom took what she offered. The eager mouth, the quick dance of her tongue against his, the kick to his pulse when her breasts flattened against his chest.

He dropped his hands, cupped her bottom and pulled her closer. A serious mistake, he realized the instant her hip gouged into his groin. Biting down a groan, he eased back an inch or two.

"I want you, Natalie. You can see it. Feel it. But…"

"I want you, too."

"But," he continued gruffly, "I'm not going to take advantage of your confusion and uncertainty."

She leaned back in his arms and considered that for several moments while Dom shifted a little to one side to ease the pressure of her hip.

"I think it's the other way around," she said at last. "I'm the one taking advantage. You didn't have to let me stay at the loft. Or go with me to Dr. Kovacs, or get a copy of my driver's license, or come with me today."

"So I was just supposed to set you adrift far from your home with no money and no identity?"

"The point is, you didn't set me adrift." Her voice softened, and her eyes misted. "You're my anchor, Dominic. My lifeline." She leaned in again and brushed his mouth with hers. "Thank you."

The soft whisper sliced into him like a double-bladed ax. Wrapping his hands around her upper arms, he pushed her away. Surprise left her slack-jawed and gaping up at him.

"Is that what this is about, Natalie? You're so grateful you feel you have to respond when I kiss you? Perhaps sleep with me in payment for services rendered?"

"No!" Indignation sent a tide of red to her cheeks. "Of all the arrogant, idiotic…"

She stopped, dragged in a breath and tilted her chin to a dangerous angle.

"I guess you didn't notice, St. Sebastian, but I happen to like kissing you. I suspect I would also like going to bed with you. But I'll be damned if I'll do it with you thinking I'm so pathetic that I should be grateful for any crumbs that you and the hound and Kissy Face Arabella and…" She waved an irate hand. "And all your other friends toss my way."

The huffy speech left Dom swinging from anger to amusement. He didn't trust himself to address her comment about Arabella. Just the thought of Natalie wearing the Londoner's black silk put another kink in his gut. The hound was a different matter.

"This is a first," he admitted. "I've never been lumped in the same category as a dog before."

"You're not in the same category," she retorted. "Duke at least recognizes honest emotions like friendship and loyalty and affection."

"Affection?" His ego dropped another notch. "That's what you feel for me?"

"Oh, for....!" Exasperated, she twisted out of his arms and planted both fists on her hips. "What do you want, *Your Highness*? A written confession that I lay awake last night wishing it was you snuffling beside me instead of Duke? An engraved invitation to take his place?"

He searched her face, her eyes, and read only indignation and frustration. No subliminal fear stemming from a traumatic past event. No prim, old-maidish reluctance to get sweaty and naked. No confusion about what she wanted.

His scruples died an instant death as hunger rushed hot and greedy through his veins. "No engraved invitation required. I'll take this." He reached for her again and found her mouth. "And this," he murmured, nipping at her throat. "And this," he growled as his hand found her breast.

When he scooped her into his arms several long, mind-drugging moments later, his conscience fought through the red haze for a last, desperate battle. She was still lost, dammit! Still vulnerable. Despite her irate speech, he shouldn't carry her to the bed.

Shouldn't, but did. Some contrary corner of his mind said it was her very vulnerability that made him want to strengthen the lifeline she mentioned. Anchor her even more securely.

The last thought shook him. Not enough to stop him,

though. Especially with the moonlight spilling through the windows, bathing her face and now well-kissed lips in a soft glow.

His hunger erupted in a greedy, gnawing need. He stood her on her feet beside the bed and peeled away her clothes with more haste than finesse. Impatience made him clumsy but fired a similar urgency in Natalie. She tugged his shirt over his head and dropped hungry kisses on his chest as she fumbled with the snap of his jeans.

When he dragged back the thick, down-filled feather-bed and tumbled her to the sheets, her body was smooth and warm, a landscape of golden lights and dark shadows. And when she hooked a calf around one of his, he had to fight the primal need to drive into her. He had to get something straight between them first. Thrusting his hands into her hair, he delivered a quick kiss and a wry confession.

"Just so you don't think this is your idea, you should know I was plotting various ways to get you into bed when I came to your hotel room in New York."

Natalie's heart kicked. In a sudden flash, she could see the small hotel room. Two double beds. An open laptop. Herself going nose to nose with Dom about… About…

"You thought I was some kind of schemer, out to fleece the duchess."

He went still. "You remember that?"

"Yes!" She clung to the image, sorting through the emotions that came with it. One proved especially satisfying. "I also remember slamming the door in your face," she said gleefully.

"You do, huh?" He got even for that with a long, hard kiss that left her gasping. "Remember anything else?"

"Not at the moment," she gulped.

He released her hair and slid his hands down her neck, over her shoulders, down her body. "Then I guess we'd better generate a few new memories."

Natalie gasped again as he set to work exploring her body. Nipping her earlobe. Kneading her breasts. Teasing her nipples. Tracing a path down her belly to the apex of her thighs. She was quivering with delight when he used a knee to part her legs.

His hair-roughened thigh rasped against hers. His breathing went fast and harsh. And his hand—his busy, diabolical hand—found her center. She was hot and wet and eager when he slid a finger in. Two. All the while his thumb played over the tight bud at her center and his teeth brought her nipples to taut, aching peaks. As the sensations piled one on top of the other, she arched under him.

"Dom! Dom, I... Ooooooh!"

The cry ripped from deep in her throat. She tried to hold back but the sensations spiraling up from her belly built to a wild, whirling vortex. Shuddering, she rode them to the last, gasping breath.

Minutes, maybe hours later, she pried up eyelids that felt as heavy as lead. Dom had propped his weight on one elbow and was watching her intently. He must be thinking of Dr. Kovacs's hypothesis, she realized. Worrying that some repressed trauma in her past might make her wig out.

"That," she assured him on a ragged sigh, "was wonderful."

His face relaxed into a smile. "Good to hear, but we're not done yet."

Still boneless with pleasure, she stretched like a cat as he rolled to the side of the bed and groped among the clothes they'd left in a pile on the floor. Somehow she wasn't surprised when he turned back with several foil-wrapped condoms. By the time he'd placed them close at hand on the table beside the bed, she was ready for round two.

"My turn," she murmured, pushing up on an elbow to

explore his body with the same attention to detail he'd explored hers.

God, he was beautiful! That wasn't an adjective usually applied to males but Natalie couldn't think of any other to categorize the long, lean torso, the roped muscle at shoulder and thigh, the flat belly and nest of thick, dark hair at his groin. His sex was flaccid but came to instant, eager attention when she stroked a finger along its length.

But it was the scar that caught and held her attention. Healed but still angry in the dim glow of the moon, it cut diagonally along his ribs. Frowning, she traced the tip of her finger along the vicious path.

"What's this?"

"A reminder not to trust a rookie to adequately pat down a seasoned veteran of the Cosa Nostra."

She spotted another scar higher on his chest, this one a tight, round pucker of flesh.

"And this?"

"A parting gift from an Albanian boat captain after Interpol intercepted the cargo of girls he was transporting to Algeria."

He said it with a careless shrug, as if knife wounds and kidnappings were routine occurrences in the career of a secret agent. Which they probably were, Natalie thought with a swallow. Suddenly the whole James Bond thing didn't seem quite so romantic.

"Your employer's brother-in-law took part in that op," Dom was saying. "Gina's husband, Jack Harris."

"He's undercover, too?"

"No, he's a career diplomat. He was part of a UN investigation into child prostitution at the time."

"Have I met him?"

"I don't know."

"Hmm."

It was hard to work up an interest in her employer's

brother-in-law while she was stretched out hip-to-naked-hip with Dominic St. Sebastian. Aching for the insults done to his body, she kissed the puckered scar on his shoulder.

One kiss led to another, then another, as she traced a path down his chest. When she laved her tongue along the scar bisecting his stomach, his belly hollowed and his sex sprang to attention again. Natalie drew a nail lightly along its length and would have explored the smooth satin further but Dom inhaled sharply and jerked away from her touch.

"Sorry! I want you too much."

She started to tell him there was no need for apologies, but he was already reaching for one of the condoms he'd left so conveniently close at hand. Heat coiled low in her belly and then, when he turned back to her, raced through her in quick, electric jolts. On fire for him, she took his weight and welcomed him eagerly into her body.

There was no slow climb to pleasure this time. No delicious heightening of the senses. He drove into her, and all too soon Natalie felt another climax rushing at her. She tried desperately to contain it, then sobbed with relief and sheer, undiluted pleasure when he pushed both her and himself over the edge.

She sprawled in naked abandon while the world slowly stopped spinning. Dom lay next to her, his eyes closed and one arm bent under his head. As she stared at his profile in the dim light of the moon, a dozen different emotions bounced between her heart and her head.

She acknowledged the satisfaction, the worry, the delight and just the tiniest frisson of fear. She hardly knew this man, yet she felt so close to him. *Too* close. How could she tell how much of that was real or the by-product of being too emotionally dependent on him?

As if to underscore her doubts, she glanced over his shoulder at the open window. Silhouetted against a midnight-blue sky were the ruins that had brought her to Hungary and to Dom.

Somehow.

The need to find the missing pieces of the puzzle put a serious dent in the sensual satisfaction of just lazing next to him. She bit her lip and shifted her attention to the desk tucked in the alcove under the eaves. Her briefcase lay atop the desk, right where she'd placed it. Anticipation tap-danced along her nerves at the thought of attacking those fat files and getting into her laptop.

Dom picked up on her quiver of impatience and opened his eyes. "Are you cold?"

"A little," she admitted but stopped him before he could drag up the down-filled featherbed tangled at their feet. "It's early yet. I'd like to go through my briefcase before we call it a night."

Amusement colored his voice. "Do you think we're done for the night?"

"Aren't we?"

"Ah, Natushka, we've barely begun. But we'll take a break while you look through your files." He rolled out of bed with the controlled grace of a panther and pulled on his clothes. "I'll go down and get us some coffee, yes?"

"Coffee would be good."

While he was gone she made a quick trip to the bathroom, then dug into her suitcase. She scrambled into clean panties but didn't bother with a bra. Or with either of the starched blouses folded atop a beige linen jumper that had all the grace and style of a burlap sack. Frowning, she checked the tag and saw the jumper was two sizes larger than the clothes she'd bought in Budapest.

Was Dom right? Had she deliberately tried to disguise her real self in these awful clothes? Was there something in her past that made her wary of showing her true colors? If so, she might find a clue to whatever it was in the briefcase. Impatient to get to it, she stuffed the jumper back in the case and slipped on the soccer shirt she'd appropriated from Dom to use as a sleep shirt. It hung below her hips but felt soft and smooth against her thighs.

She lifted the files out of her briefcase and arranged them in neat stacks. She was flipping through one page by page when Dom returned with two mugs of foaming latte.

"Finding anything interesting?" he asked as he set a mug at her elbow.

"Tons of stuff! So far it all relates to missing works of art, like that Fabergé egg and a small Bernini bronze stolen from the Uffizi Gallery in Florence. I haven't found information on the Canaletto painting yet. It's got to be in one of these files, though."

He nodded to the still-closed laptop. "You probably cross-indexed the paper files on your computer. Why don't you check it?"

"I tried." She blew out a frustrated breath. "The laptop's password-protected."

"And you can't remember the password."

"I tried a dozen different combinations, but none worked."

"Do you want me to get into it?"

"How can you…? Oh. Another useful skill you picked up at Interpol, right?"

He merely smiled. "Do you have a USB cord in your briefcase? Good. Let me have it."

He deposited the latte on the table beside the easy chair and settled in with the computer on his lap. It booted up to a smiley face and eight blinking question marks in the password box. Dom plugged one end of the USB cord into the laptop, the other into his cell phone. He tapped a series of numbers on the phone's keypad and waited to connect via a secure remote link to a special program developed by Interpol's Computer Crimes Division for use by agents in the field. The handy-dandy program whizzed through hundreds of thousands of letter/number/character combinations at the speed of light.

Scant minutes later, the password popped up letter by letter. Dom made a note of it and hit Return. The smiley face on Natalie's laptop dissolved and the home screen came up. The icons were arranged with military precision, he saw with an inner smile. God forbid his fussy archivist should keep a messy electronic filing cabinet. He was about to tell Natalie that he was in when a message painted across the screen.

D—I see you're online. Don't know whose computer you're using. Contact me. I have some info for you. A.

About time! Dom erased the message and de-linked before passing the laptop to Natalie. "You're good to go."

She took it eagerly and wedged it onto the desk between the stacks of paper files. Fingers flying, she conducted a quick search.

"Here's the Canaletto folder!"

A click of the mouse opened the main file. When dozens of subfolders rippled down the screen, Natalie groaned.

"It'll take all night to go through these."

"You don't have all night," Dom warned, dropping a kiss on her nape. "Just till I get back."

"Where are you going?"

"I need to let Katya and her father know we won't be home tonight. I'll get a stronger signal outside."

It wasn't a complete lie. He did need to call his downstairs neighbors. That bit about the stronger signal shaded the truth, but the habit of communicating privately with his contacts at headquarters went too deep to compromise.

He slipped on a jacket and went downstairs. The bar was still open. Lisel waved, inviting him in for another coffee or a beer, but he shook his head and held up his phone to signal his reason for going outside.

He'd forgotten how sharp and clean and cold the nights could be here in the foothills of the Alps. And how bright the stars were without a haze of smog and city lights to blur them. Hiking up the collar of his jacket, he contacted Andre.

"What have you got for me?"

"Some interesting information about your Natalie Elizabeth Clark."

Dom's stomach tightened. "Interesting" to Andre could mean anything from an unpaid speeding ticket to enrollment in a witness protection program.

"It took a while, but the facial recognition program finally matched to a mug shot."

Hell! His gut had told him Natalie was hiding her real self. He almost didn't want to hear the reason behind the disguise now but forced himself to ask.

"What were the charges?"

"Fraud and related activities in connection with computers."

"When?" he bit out.

"Three years ago. But it looks like the charges were dropped and the arrest record expunged. Someone missed the mug shot, though, when they wiped the slate."

Dom wanted to be fair. The fact that the charges had been dropped could mean the arrest was a mistake, that Natalie hadn't done whatever the authorities thought she had. Unfortunately, he'd seen too many sleazy, high-priced lawyers spring their clients on technicalities.

"Do you want me to contact the feds in the US?" Andre asked. "See what they've got on this?"

Dom hesitated, his gaze going to the brightly illuminated window on the second floor of the gasthaus. Had he just made love to a hacker? Had she tracked him down,

devised a ploy to show up at his loft dripping wet and helpless? Was this whole amnesia scene part of some elaborate sting?

Every one of his instincts screamed no. She couldn't
have faked the panic and confusion he'd glimpsed in her
eyes. Or woven a web of lies and deceit, then flamed in his
arms the way she had. The question now was whether he
could trust his instincts.

"Dom? What do you want me to do?"

He went with his gut. "Hang loose, Andre. If I need
more, I'll get back to you."

He disconnected, hoping to hell he wasn't thinking with
the wrong head, and made a quick call to his downstairs
neighbors.

Ten

Natalie was still hard at it when Dom went back upstairs. Her operation had spread from the desk to the armchair and the bed, which was now neatly remade. With pillows fluffed and the corners of the counterpane squared, he noted wryly. He also couldn't help noticing how her fingers flew over the laptop's keyboard.

"How's it coming?" he asked.

"So-so. The good news is I'm now remembering many of these details. The bad news is that I went through the Canaletto folder page by page. I also searched its corresponding computer file. I didn't find an entry that would explain why I drove down from Vienna, nor any reference to Győr or Budapest. Nothing to tell me why I hopped on a riverboat and ended up in the Danube." Sighing, she flapped a hand at the stacks now spread throughout the room. "I hope I find something in one of those."

Dom eyed the neat array of files. "How have you separated them?"

"The ones on the chair contain paper copies of documents and reports of lost art from roughly the same period as the Canaletto. The ones on the bed detail the last known locations of various missing pieces from other periods."

"Sorted alphabetically by continent and country, I see."

She looked slightly offended. "Of course. I thought I might have stumbled across something in reports from a gallery or museum or private collection that gained a new acquisition at approximately the same time the Canaletto disappeared from Karlenburgh Castle."

"What about information unrelated to missing art treasures? Any personal data in the files or on the computer that triggered memories?"

"Plenty," she said with a small sigh. "Apparently I'm as anal about my personal life as I am about professional matters. I've got everything on spreadsheets. The service record for my car. The books I've read and want to read. Checking and savings accounts. A household inventory with purchase dates, cost, serial numbers where appropriate. Restaurants I've tried, sorted by type of food and my rating. In short," she finished glumly, "my entire existence. Precise, well-organized and soulless."

She looked so frustrated, so dejected and lost, that Dom had to fight the urge to take her in his arms. He'd get into the computer later, when she was asleep, and check out the household inventory and bank accounts. Right now he was more interested in her responses to his careful probing.

"How about your email? Find anything there?"

"Other than some innocuous correspondence from people I've tagged in my address book as 'acquaintances,' everything relates to work." Her shoulders slumped. "Is my life pathetic, or what?"

If she was acting, she was the best he'd ever seen. To hell with fighting the urge. She needed comforting. Clearing the armchair, he caught her hand and tugged her into his lap.

"There's more to you than spreadsheets and color-coded files, Ms. Clark."

With another sigh, she laid her head on his shoulder. "You'd think so."

"There are all your little quirks," he said with a smile,

stroking her hair. "The lip thing, the fussiness, the questionable fashion sense."

"Gee, thanks."

"Then there's your rapport with the Agár."

"Ha! I suspect he bonds instantly with everyone."

"And there's tonight," he reminded her. "You, me, this gasthaus."

She tipped her head back to search his face. He supported her head, careful of the still-tender spot at the base of her skull.

"About tonight... You, me, this place..."

"Don't look so worried. We don't have to analyze or dissect what happened here."

"I'm thinking more along the lines of what happens after we leave. Next week. Next month."

"We let them take care of themselves."

As soon as he said it, he knew it was a lie. Despite the mystery surrounding this woman—or maybe because of it—he had no intention of letting her drop out of his life the same way she'd dropped into it. She was under his skin now.

That last thought made him stop. Rewind. Take a breath. Think about the other women he'd been with. The hard, inescapable fact was that none of them had ever stirred this particular mix of lust, tenderness, worry, suspicion and fierce protectiveness.

He might have to change his tactics if and when Natalie's memory fully returned, Dom acknowledged. At the moment she considered him an anchor in a sea of uncertainty. He couldn't add to that uncertainty by demanding more than she was ready to give.

"For now," he said with a lazy smile, "this is good, isn't it?"

"Oh, yes."

She leaned in, brought her mouth to his, gave him a

promise of things to come. He was ready to take her up on that promise when she made a brisk announcement.

"Okay, I'm done wallowing in self-pity. Time to get back to work."

"What do you want me to do?"

She glanced at the files on the bed and caught her lower lip between her teeth. Dom waited, remembering how antsy she'd been about letting him see her research when he'd shown up unannounced at her New York hotel room. He'd chalked that up to a proprietary desire to protect her work. With Andre's call still fresh in his mind, he couldn't help wondering if there was something else in those fat folders she wanted to protect.

"I guess you could start on those," she said with obvious reluctance. "There's an index and a chronology inside each file. The sections are tabbed, the documents in each section numbered. That's how I cross-reference the contents on the computer. So keep everything in order, okay?"

Dom's little bubble of suspicion popped. The woman wasn't nervous about him digging into her private files, just worried that he'd mess them up. Grinning, he pushed out of the chair with her still in his arms and deposited her back at the desk.

"I'll treat every page with care and reverence," he promised solemnly.

She flushed at little at the teasing but stood her ground. "You'd better. We archivists don't take kindly to anyone who desecrates our files."

It didn't take Dom long to realize Natalie could land a job with any investigative agency in the world, including Interpol. She hadn't just researched facts about lost cultural treasures. She'd tracked every rumor, followed every thread. Some threads were so thin they appeared to have no relation to the object of her research. Yet in at least two of the files he dug through, those seemingly unrelated, unconnected tidbits of information led to a major find.

"Jesus," Dom muttered after following a particularly convoluted trail. "Do you remember this?"

She swiveled around and frowned at a scanned photo depicting a two-inch-long cylinder inscribed with hieroglyphics. "Looks familiar. It's Babylonian, isn't it? About two thousand years old, I'd guess."

"You'd guess right."

"What's the story on it?"

"It went missing in Iraq in 2003, shortly after Saddam Hussein was toppled."

"Oh, I remember now. I found a reference to a similar object in a list of items being offered for sale by a little-known dealer. Best I recall, he claimed he specialized in Babylonian artifacts."

She rubbed her forehead, trying to dredge up more detail. Dom helped her out.

"You sent him a request for a more detailed description of that particular item. When it came in, you matched it to a list the US Army compiled of Iraqi antiquities that were unaccounted for."

"I can't remember...did the army recover the artifact?"

He flipped through several pages of notes and correspondence. "They did. They also arrested the contractor employee who'd lifted it during recovery efforts at the Baghdad Archeological Museum."

"Well! Maybe I'm not so pathetic after all."

She turned back to the laptop with a smug little smile that crushed the last of Dom's doubts. Those two inches of inscribed Babylonian clay were damned near priceless. If Natalie was into shady deals, she wouldn't have alerted the army to her find. The fact that she had convinced Dom. Whatever screwup had led to her arrest, she was no hacker or huckster.

He dug into the next folder and soon found himself absorbed in the search for a thirteenth-century gold chalice studded with emeralds that once graced the altar of an Irish abbey. He was only halfway through the thick file when he glanced up and saw Natalie's shoulders drooping again, this time with fatigue. So much for his anticipation of another lively session under the featherbed. He closed the folder, careful not to dislodge any of its contents, and stretched.

"That's it for me tonight."

She frowned at the remaining files. "We've still got a half dozen to go through."

"Tomorrow. Right now, I need bed, sleep and you. Not necessarily in that order, although you look as whipped as I feel."

"I might be able to summon a few reserves of energy."

"You do that," he said as he headed for the bathroom.

His five-o'clock shadow had morphed into a ten-o'clock bristle. He'd scraped Natalie's tender cheeks enough the first time around. He better shave and go a little more gentle on her this time. But when he reentered the bedroom a scant ten minutes later, she was curled in a tight ball under the featherbed and sawing soft, breathy Z's.

Taking advantage of the opportunity, he settled at the desk. His conscience didn't even ping as he powered up her laptop. Forty minutes later he'd seen everything he needed to. His skills weren't as honed as those of the wizards in Interpol's Computer Crimes Division, but they were good enough for him to feel confident she wasn't hacking into unauthorized databases or shifting money into hidden accounts. Everything he saw indicated she'd lived well within her salary as an archivist for the State of Illinois and was now socking most of the generous salary Sarah paid her into a savings account.

Satisfied and more than a little relieved to have his instincts validated, Dom shed his clothes and slid in beside her lax, warm body. He was tempted to nudge her awake and treat himself to a celebration of his nonfindings. He restrained himself but it required a heroic effort.

Natalie woke to bright morning sunshine, the distant clang of cowbells and a feeling of energy and purpose. She ascribed the last to a solid night's sleep—until she tried to roll over and realized she probably owed it more to the solid wall of male behind her.

God, he felt good! What's more, he made *her* feel good. Just lying nested against his warmth and strength generated all kinds of wild possibilities. Like maybe waking up in the same nest for the next few weeks or months. Or even, her sneaky little subconscious suggested, years.

The thought struck her that Dominic St. Sebastian might be all she needed to feel complete. All she would ever need. Apparently, she had no family. Judging by the dearth of personal emails on her laptop, she didn't have a wide circle of friends. Yet lying here with Dom, she didn't feel the lack of either.

Maybe that's why the details of her personal life were so slow returning. Her life was so empty, so blah, she didn't *want* to remember it. That made her grimace, which must have translated into some small movement because a lazy voice sounded just behind her ear.

"I've been waiting for you to wake up."

Sheets rustling, she angled a look over her shoulder and sighed. "It's not fair."

"What isn't?"

"My eyes feel goopy from sleep, my hair's probably sticking out in all directions and I know my teeth need brushing. You, on the other hand, look fresh and wide-awake and good enough to eat."

Good enough to gobble whole, actually. Those black

eyes and hair, the golden-oak hue of his skin, the square chin and chiseled cheekbones…the whole package added up to something really spectacular to start the day with. Only the nicks and scars of his profession marred the perfection.

"In fact," she announced, "I think I'll have you for breakfast."

She rolled onto her side, trying not to treat him to a blast of morning breath, and wiggled down a few inches. She started with the underside of his jaw and slowly worked her way south. Teasing, tasting, nibbling the cords in his neck, dropping kisses on alternate ribs, circling his belly button with her tongue. By the time she dragged the sheets down to his hips, he was stiff and rampant.

Her own belly tight and quivering now, she circled him with her palm. The skin was hot and satin smooth, the blood throbbing in his veins. She slid her hand up, down, up again, delighted when he grunted and jerked involuntarily.

"Okay," she told him, her voice throaty with desire, "I need a little of that action."

All thought of ratty hair and goopy eyes forgotten, she swung a leg over his thighs and raised her hips. Dom was straining and eager but held her off long enough to tear into another foil package.

"Let me," she said, brushing his hands aside.

She rolled on the condom, then positioned her hips again. Together they rode to an explosive release that had him thrusting upward and her collapsing onto his chest in mindless, mewling pleasure.

Natalie recovered first. Probably because she had to pee really, really bad. She scooped up her jeans and the green-and-white-striped rugby shirt she now claimed as her own on the way to the bathroom. When she emerged, she found Dom dressed and waiting for his turn.

"Give me five minutes and I'll be ready to go."

Since she wasn't sure whether they would return to the gasthaus, she stuffed the files and laptop back into her briefcase and threw her few miscellaneous items into her weekender. The sight of those plain, sensible, neatly folded blouses made her wrinkle her nose. Whatever happened when—*if*—she regained her memory, she was investing in an entire new wardrobe.

Dom agreed that it was probably better to check out of the gasthaus and head back to Budapest after going up to the castle. "But first, we'll eat. I guarantee you've never tasted anything like Lisel's *bauernfrühstück*."

"Which is?"

"Her version of a German-Austrian-Hungarian farmer's breakfast."

Their hostess gave them a cheerful smile when they appeared in the dining room and waved them to a table. She was serving two other diners, locals by the looks of them, and called across the room.

"Frühstück, ja?"

"Ja," Dom called back as he and Natalie helped themselves to the coffee and fresh juice set out on an elaborately carved hutch.

A short time later Lisel delivered her special. Natalie gaped at the platter-size omelette bursting with fried potatoes, onions, leeks, ham and pungent Munster cheese. The Hungarian input came from the pulpy, stewed tomatoes flavored with red peppers and the inevitable paprika.

When their hostess returned with a basket of freshly baked rolls and a crock of homemade elderberry jam, she lingered long enough to knuckle Dom's shoulder affectionately.

"So you leave us today?"

His mouth full, Dom nodded.

"You must come again soon." The blonde's amethyst eyes twinkled as she included his companion in the invitation. "You, as well. You and Dominic found the bed in my front room comfortable, yes?"

Natalie could feel heat rushing into her cheeks but had to laugh. "Very comfortable."

With a respectable portion of her gargantuan breakfast disposed of and the innkeeper's warm farewells to speed them on their way, Natalie's spirits rose with every twist and turn of the road that snaked up to the mountain pass. Something had drawn her to the ruins dominating the skyline ahead. She felt it in her bones, in the excitement bubbling through her veins. Impatience had her straining against her seat belt as Dom turned off the main road onto the single lane that led to what was left of Karlenburgh Castle.

The lane had once been paved but over the years frost heaves had buckled the asphalt and weeds now sprouted in the cracks. The weedy approach took nothing away from the dramatic aspect of the ruins, however. They rose from a base of solid granite, looking as though they'd been carved from the mountain itself. To the west was a breath-stealing vista of the snow-covered Austrian Alps. To the east, a series of stair-stepping terraces that must once have contained gardens, vineyards and orchards. The terraces ended abruptly in a sheer drop to the valley below.

Natalie's heart was pounding by the time Dom pulled up a few yards from the outer wall. The wind slapped her in the face when she got out of the car and knifed through the rugby shirt.

"Here, put this on."

Dom held up the jacket he'd retrieved from the backseat. She slid her arms into the sleeves and wrapped its warmth around her gratefully.

"Watch your step," he warned as they approached a gap in the outer ring of rubble. "A massive portcullis used to guard this gate, but the Soviets claimed the iron for scrap—along with everything else of any value. Then," he said, his voice grim, "they set charges and destroyed the castle itself as a warning to other Hungarians foolish enough to join the uprising."

Someone had cleared a path through the rubble of the outer bailey. "My grandfather," Dom explained, "with help from some locals."

Grasping her elbow to guide her over the rough spots, he pointed out the charred timbers and crumpled walls of the dairy, what had been the kitchens in earlier centuries, and the stables-turned-carriage house and garage.

Another gate led to what would have been the inner courtyard. The rubble was too dense here to penetrate but she could see the outline of the original structure in the tumbled walls. The only remaining turret jutted up like a broken tooth, its roof blown and stone staircase exposed to the sky. Natalie hooked her arm through Dom's and let her gaze roam the desolation while he described the castle he himself had seen only in drawings and family photographs.

"Karlenburgh wasn't as large as some border fortresses of the same era. Only thirty-six rooms originally, including the armory, the great hall and the duke and duchess's chambers. Successive generations of St. Sebastians installed modern conveniences like indoor plumbing and electric lights, but for comfort and luxury the family usually wintered in their palazzos on the Italian Riviera or the Dalmatian Coast." A smile lightened his somber expression. "My grandfather had a photo of him and his cousin dunking each other in the Mediterranean. They were very close as children, he and the last Grand Duke."

"Except," Natalie said, squeezing his arm with hers, "he wasn't the last Grand Duke."

For once Dominic didn't grimace or shrug or otherwise downplay his heritage. He couldn't, with its very dramatic remains staring him in the face.

"I've told the duchess she should come back for a visit," he murmured almost to himself. "But seeing it like this…"

They stood with shoulders hunched against the wind, Dom thinking of the duchess and Natalie searching the ruins for something to jog her memory. What had drawn her here? What had she found among the rubble that propelled her from here to Győr and onto that damned boat?

It was there, just behind the veil. She knew it was there! But she was damned if she could pull it out. Disappointment ate into her, doubly sharp and bitter after her earlier excitement.

Dom glanced down and must have read the frustration in her face. "Nothing?" he asked gently.

"Just a sort of vague, prickly sensation," she admitted, "which may or may not be goose bumps raised by the cold."

"Whichever it is, we'd best get you out of the wind."

Dejected and deflated and feeling dangerously close to tears, she picked her way back through the rubble. She'd been so sure Karlenburgh Castle was the key. So certain she'd break through once she stood among the ruins.

Lost in her glum thoughts, her eyes on the treacherous path, it took a moment for a distant, tinny clanging to penetrate her preoccupation. When it did, her head jerked up. That sound! That metallic tinkling! She'd heard it before, and not long ago.

Her heart started pumping. Her mouth went dry. Feeling as though she was teetering on the edge of a precipice, she followed the clanging to a string of goats meandering along the overgrown lane in their direction. A gnarled gnome of a man trailed the flock. His face was shadowed by the wide brim of his hat and he leaned heavily on a burled wood staff.

"That's old Friedrich," Dom exclaimed. "He helped tend the castle's goats as a small boy and now raises his own. Those are *cou noirs*—black necks—especially noted for their sweet milk. My grandfather always stopped by Friedrich's hut to buy cheese when he brought Zia and me back for a visit."

Natalie stood frozen as Dom forged a path through the goats to greet their herder. She didn't move, couldn't! Even when the lead animals milled inquisitively around her knees. True to their name, their front quarters were black, the rest of their coat a grayish-white. The does were gentle creatures but some instinct told Natalie to keep a wary eye on the buck accompanying them.

A bit of trivia slipped willy-nilly into her mind. She'd read somewhere that Alpine goats were among the earliest domesticated animals. Also that their adaptability made them good candidates for long sea voyages. Early settlers in the Americas had brought this breed with them to supply milk and cheese. And sea captains would often leave a pair on deserted islands along their trade routes to provide fresh milk and meat on return voyages.

Suddenly, the curtains in her mind parted. Not all the way. Just far enough for her to know she hadn't picked up that bit of trivia "somewhere." She'd specifically researched Alpine goats on Google after... After...

Her gaze shot to the herder hobbling alongside Dom, a smile on his wrinkled walnut of a face. Excitement rushed back, so swift and thrilling she was shaking with it when Friedrich smiled and greeted her in a mix of German and heavily accented English.

"*Guten tag, fraülein. Es gut* to see you again."

Eleven

Natalie had spent all those hours soul- and mind- and computer-searching. She'd tried desperately to latch on to something, *anything*, that would trigger her memory. Never in her wildest dreams would she have imagined that trigger would consist of a herd of smelly goats and a wizened little man in a floppy felt hat. Yet the moment Friedrich greeted her in his fractured English, the dam broke.

Images flooded the empty spaces in her mind. Her, standing almost on this same spot. The goatherd, inquiring kindly if she was lost. These same gray-white does butting her knees. The buck giving her the evil eye. A casual chat that sent her off on a wild chase.

"*Guten tag*, Herr Müller." Her voice shook with excitement. "*Es gut* to see you again, too."

Dom had already picked up on the goatherd's greeting to Natalie. Her reply snapped his brows together. "When did you and Friedrich meet?"

"A week ago! Right here, at the castle! I remember him, Dom. I remember the goats and the bells and Herr Müller asking if I was lost. Then…then…"

She was so close to hyperventilating she had to stop and drag in a long, hiccuping breath. Müller looked confused by the rapid-fire exchange, so Natalie forced herself to slow down, space the words, contain the hysterical joy that bubbled to the surface.

"Then we sat there, on that wall, and you told me about the castle before the Soviets came. About the balls and the hunting parties and the tree-lighting ceremony in the great hall. Everyone from the surrounding villages was invited, you said. On Christmas Eve. Uh...*Heiliger Abend*."

"Ja, ja, Heiliger Abend."

"When I mentioned that I'd met the duchess in New York, you told me that you remember when she came to Karlenburgh Castle as a bride. So young and beautiful and gracious to everyone, even the knock-kneed boy who helped tend the goats."

She had to stop and catch her breath again. She could see the scene from last week so clearly now, every detail as though etched in glass. The weeds poking from the cracks in the road. The goats wandering through the rubble. This hunched-shouldered man in his gray felt hat, his gnarled hands folded atop the head of his walking stick, describing Karlenburgh Castle in its glory days.

"Then," she said, the excitement piling up again, "I told you I was searching for a painting that had once hung in the Red Salon. You gave me a very hard look and asked why I, too, should want to know about that particular room after all these years."

Everything was coming at her so fast and furiously and seemingly in reverse, like a DVD rewound at superhigh speed. The encounter with Herr Müller. The drive down from Vienna. A burning curiosity to see the castle ruins. The search for the Canaletto. Sarah and Dev. The duchess and Gina and the twins and Anastazia and meeting Dom for the first time in New York.

The rewind came to a screeching halt, stuck at that meeting with Dom. She could see his laughing eyes. His lazy grin. Hear his casual dismissal of the codicil and the title it conferred on him.

That was one of the reasons she'd returned to Vienna!

Why she'd decided to make a day trip to view the ruins of Karlenburgh Castle, and why she'd been so blasted determined to track the missing Canaletto. She'd wanted to wipe that cynical smile off Dominic St. Sebastian's face. Prove the validity of her research. Rub his nose in it, in fact. And, oh, by the way, possibly determine what happened to a priceless work of art.

And why, when the police tried to determine who she was and what she was doing in Budapest, the only response she could dredge from her confused mind was the Grand Duke of Karlenburgh!

With a fierce effort of will, she sidelined those tumultuous memories and focused on the goatherd. "I asked you who else had enquired about the Red Salon. Remember? You told me someone had come some months ago. And told you his name."

"Ja." His wrinkled face twisting in disgust, Müller aimed a thick wad of spittle at the ground. "Janos Lagy."

Dom had been listening intently without interruption to this point, but the name the goatherd spit out provoked a startled response. "Janos Lagy?"

Natalie threw him a surprised glance but he whipped up a palm and stilled the question she saw quivering on her lips.

"Ja," Müller continued in his thick, accented English. "Janos Lagy, a banker, he tells me, from Budapest. He tells me, too, he is the grandson of a Hungarian who goes to the military academy in Moscow and becomes a *mladshij lejtenant* in the Soviet Army. And I tell him I remember this lieutenant," the goatherd related, his voice shaking with emotion. "He commands the squad sent to destroy Karlenburgh Castle after the Grand Duke is arrested."

Dom mumbled something in Hungarian under his breath. Something short and terse and sounding very unnice to Natalie. She ached to ask him what he knew about

Lagy but Herr Müller was just getting to the crux of the story he'd shared with her less than a week ago.

"When I tell this to the grandson, he shrugs. He shrugs, the grandson of this traitorous lieutenant, as if it's of no matter, and asks me if I am ever in the Red Salon!"

The old man quivered with remembered rage. Raising his walking stick, he shook it in the air.

"I threatened to knock his head. He leaves very quickly then."

"Jézus," Dom muttered. "Janos Lagy."

Natalie couldn't contain herself. "You know him?"

"I know him."

"How!"

"I'll explain in the car, and you can tell me what you did with the information Friedrich gave you. But first…"

He probed for more information but when it was clear the goatherd had shared all he knew, he started to take a gracious leave. To his surprise and acute embarrassment, the old man grabbed his hand and kissed it.

"The Grand Duke and Duchess, they are still missed here," he said with tears swimming in his eyes. "It's good, what I read in the papers, that you are now duke. You'll come back again? Soon?"

"I will," he promised. "And perhaps I can convince the duchess to come, too."

"Ahhhh, I pray that I live to see her again!"

They left him clinging to that hope and picked their way through the weeds back to the car. Natalie was a quivering bundle of nerves but the deep crease between Dom's eyes kept her silent while he keyed the ignition, maneuvered a tight turn and regained the road that snaked up and over the pass. Neither of them spoke until he pulled into a scenic turnout that gave an eagle's-eye view of the valley below.

When Dom swung toward her, his face was still tight. "Start at the beginning. Tell what you remember."

She rewound the DVD again. She focused her growing absorption with both the codicil and Canaletto but glossed over the ignoble desire to rub a certain someone's nose in her research.

"I was there in Vienna, only a little over an hour away. I wanted to see the castle the duchess had told me about during our interviews, perhaps talk to some locals who might remember her."

"Like Friedrich Müller."

"Like Friedrich Müller," she confirmed. "I'd done a review of census records and knew he was one of only a handful of people old enough to have lived through the 1956 Uprising. I intended to go to the address listed as his current residence, but met him by chance there at the ruins instead."

"What a string of coincidences," Dom muttered, shaking his head. "Incredible."

"Not really," she countered, defensive on behalf of her research. "Pretty much everything one needs to know is documented somewhere. You just have to look for it."

He conceded the point. "So you met Friedrich, and he told you about Lagy. What did you do then?"

"I researched him on Google as soon as I got back to my hotel in Vienna. Took me a while to find the right Lagy. It's a fairly common name in Hungary. But I finally tracked him to his office at his bank. His secretary wouldn't put me through until I identified myself as Sarah St. Sebastian Hunter's research assistant and said I was helping with her book dealing with lost works of art. Evidently Janos is something of a collector. He came on the line a few minutes later."

"Did you tell him you were trying to track the Canaletto?"

"Yes, and he asked why I'd contacted him about it. I didn't want to go into detail over the phone, just said I thought I'd found a possible link through his grandfather that I'd like to pursue with him. He asked if I'd discussed this link with anyone else and I told him no, that I wanted to verify it first. I offered to drive to Budapest but he generously offered to meet me halfway."

"In Győr."

"On the tour boat," she confirmed. "He said cruising the Danube was one of his favorite ways to relax, that if I hadn't taken a day trip on the river before I would most certainly enjoy it. I knew I wouldn't. I hate boats, loathe being on the water. But I was so eager to talk to him I agreed. I drove down to Győr the next day."

"And you met Lagy aboard?"

"No. He called after the damned boat had left the dock and said he'd been unavoidably detained. He apologized profusely and said he would meet me when it docked in Budapest instead."

She made a moue of distaste, remembering the long, queasy hours trying not to fixate on the slap of the current against the hull or the constant engine vibration under her feet.

"We didn't approach Budapest until late afternoon. By then I was huddled at the rail near the back of the boat, praying I wouldn't be sick. I remember getting another call. Remember reaching too fast for my phone and feeling really dizzy. I leaned over the rail, thinking I was going to puke." Frowning, she slid her hand under her hair and fingered the still tender spot at the base of her skull. "I must have banged my head on one of the support poles because there was pain. Nasty, nasty pain. And the next thing I know someone's leaning on my chest, pumping water out of my lungs!"

"You never saw Janos Lagy? Never connected with him?"

"Not unless he was one of the guys who fished me out of the river. Who *is* he, Dom? How do you know him?"

"We went to school together."

"You're friends with him?" she asked incredulously.

"Acquaintances. My grandfather was not one to forgive or forget old wrongs. He knew Jan's grandfather had served in the Soviet Army and didn't want me to have anything to do with the Lagy family. He didn't know the bastard had commanded the squad that leveled Karlenburgh Castle, though. I didn't either, until today."

Natalie had been certain that once she regained her memory, every blank space would fill and every question would have an answer. Instead, all new questions were piling up.

"This is so frustrating." She shook her head. "Like a circle that doesn't quite close. You, me, the duchess, the castle, the painting, this guy Lagy. They're all connected, but I can't see how they come together."

"Nor do I," he said, digging his cell phone out of his jeans pocket, "but I intend to find out."

She watched wide-eyed as he pressed a single key and was instantly connected. She understood just enough of his fluid French to grasp that he was asking someone named Andre to run a check on Janos Lagy.

Their return sent the hound into a paroxysm of delight. When Natalie laughed and bent to accept his joyous adulation, he got several quick, slurpy kisses past her guard before she could dodge them.

As a thank-you to the dog-sitters, Dom gave Katya the green light to purchase the latest Justin Bieber CD on his iTunes account and download it to her iPod—with her father's permission, he added. The indulgent papa received the ten-pound Westphalia ham that Dom had picked up at the butcher's on the way home. The hound got a bag of bones, which tantalized him all the way up to the loft.

When Dom unlocked the front door and stood aside for Natalie to precede him, she was hit with a sudden attack of nerves. Now that she'd remembered her past, would it overshadow the present? Would the weight of all those months and years in her "real" life smother the brief days she'd spent here, with Dom?

Her heart thumping, she stepped inside and felt instant relief. And instantly at home…despite the dust motes dancing on a stray sunbeam and the rumpled bedcovers she'd straightened so meticulously before the hound had pounced on them. She knew she was just a guest, yet the most ridiculous sense of belonging enveloped her. The big fat question mark now was how long she'd stay camped out here. At least until she and Dom explored this business with Lagy, surely.

Or not. Doubt raised its ugly head when she glanced over her shoulder and saw him standing just inside the still-open door.

"Aren't you coming in?"

He gave himself a little shake, as if dragging his thoughts together, and dredged up a crooked smile.

"We left your case in the car. I'll go get it."

She used his absence to open the drapes and windows to let in the crisp fall air. Conscious of how Dom had teased her about her neat streak, she tried to ignore the rumpled bed but the damned thing pulled her like a magnet. She was guiltily smoothing the cover when he returned.

Propping her roller case next to the wardrobe, he made for the fridge. "I'm going to have a beer. Would you like one? Or wine, or tea?"

"Tea sounds good. Why don't I brew a fresh pitcher while you check with your friend to see what he's turned up on Lagy?"

Dom took the dew-streaked pilsner and cell phone out to the balcony. Not because he wanted privacy to make the call to Andre. He'd decided last night to trust Natalie in spite of that unexplained arrest and nothing had happened since to change his mind. Unless whatever he learned about Lagy was classified "eyes only," he intended to share it with her. No, he just needed a few moments to sort through everything that had happened in the past twenty-four hours.

Oh hell, who was he kidding?

What he needed was, first, a deep gulp of air. Second, a long swallow of Gold Fassl. And third, a little more time to recover from the mule kick that'd slammed into his midsection when he'd opened the door to the loft and Natalie waltzed in with the Agár frisking around her legs.

He liked having her here. Oddly, she didn't crowd him or shrink his loft to minuscule proportions the way Zia did whenever she blew into Budapest on one of her whirlwind visits, leaving a trail of clothes and scarves and medical books and electronic gadgets in her wake. In fact, Natalie might lean a bit too far in the opposite direction. She would alphabetize and color-code his life if he didn't keep a close eye on her.

He would have to loosen her up. Ratchet her passion for order and neatness down to human levels. He suspected that might take some work but he could manage it. All he had to do was take her to bed often enough—and keep her there long enough—to burn up any surplus energy.

As he gazed at the ornate facades on the Pest side of the river, he could easily envision fall rolling into winter while he lazed under the blankets with Natalie and viewed these same buildings dusted with snow. Or the two of them exercising the hound when the park below was tender and green with spring.

The problem was that he wasn't sure how Natalie felt

about resuming her real life now that she'd remembered it. He suspected she wasn't sure, either. Not yet, anyway. His conscience said he should stick to the suggestion he'd made last night to take things between them slowly, step-by-step. But his conscience couldn't stand up to the homey sounds of Natalie moving around inside the loft, brewing her tea, laughing at the hound's antics.

He wanted her here, with him. Wanted to show her more of the city he loved. Wanted to explore that precise, fascinating mind, hear her breathy gasps and groans when they made love.

And, he thought, his eyes going cold and flat, he wanted to flatten whoever'd hurt her. He didn't believe for a moment she'd hit her head on a support pole and tumbled into the Danube. Janos Lagy had lured her onto that tour boat and Dom was damned well going to find out why.

For once Andre didn't have the inside scoop. Instead, he referred Dom back to the Hungarian agency that conducted internal investigations. The individual Dom spoke to there was cautious and closemouthed and unwilling to share sensitive information with someone she didn't know. She did, however, agree to meet with him and Natalie in the morning.

That made two appointments for tomorrow—one at the US Embassy to obtain a replacement passport and one at the National Tax and Customs Administration.

"Tax and Customs?" Natalie echoed when he told her about the appointments. "Is that like the Internal Revenue Service in the US?"

"More like your IRS and Department of the Treasury combined. The NTCA is our focus for all financial matters, including criminal activities like money laundering and financing terrorist activities."

Her eyes rounded. "And they have something on Lagy?"

"They wouldn't say, but they're interested in talking to you."

"I can't tell them any more than I told you."

"No, but they can tell us what, if anything, Lagy's involved in."

"Well, this has been an amazing day. Two days, actually." Her eyes met his in a smile. "And a pretty amazing night."

The smile clinched it. No way was he letting this woman waltz out of his life the same way she'd waltzed in. Dom thought seriously about plucking the glass out of her hand and carrying her to the bed. Which he would, he promised himself. Later. Right now, he'd initiate a blitz-style campaign to make her develop a passion for all things Hungarian—himself included.

"Did you bring a bathing suit?"

She blinked at the abrupt change of topic. "A bathing suit?"

"Do you have one in your suitcase?"

"I packed for business, not splashing around in hotel pools."

"No matter. We can rent one."

"Rent a bathing suit?" Her fastidious little nose wrinkled. "I don't think so."

"They're sanitized and steam-cleaned. Trust me on this. Stuff a couple of towels in your tote while I feed the hound and we'll go."

"Dom, I don't think public bathing is really my thing."

"You can't leave Budapest without experiencing what gives this city its most distinctive character. Why do you think the Romans called their settlement here Aquincum?"

"Meaning water something?"

"Meaning abundant waters. All they had to do was poke a stick in the ground and a hot spring bubbled up. Get the towels."

* * *

Natalie was even less sure about the whole communal spa thing when they arrived at the elegant Gellért Hotel. The massive complex sat at the base of Gellért Hill, named, Dom informed her, for the unfortunate bishop who came from Venice at the request of King Istivan in 1000 A.D.

"My rebellious Magyar ancestors took exception to the king's conversion to Christianity," Dom related as he escorted her to the columned and colonnaded entrance. "They put the bishop in a barrel, drove long spikes in it and rolled him down the hill."

"Lovely."

"Here we go."

He ushered her into a grand entry hall two or three stories high. A long row of ticket windows lining one side of the hall offered a bewildering smorgasbord of options. Dom translated a menu that included swimming pools, thermal baths with temperatures ranging from a comfortable 86 degrees to a scorching 108 degrees, whirlpools, wave pools, saunas and steam rooms. And massages! Every sort of massage. Natalie gave up trying to pick out options and left the choice to him.

"Don't you need to know what bathing suit size I need?" she asked as they approached a ticket booth.

He cut her an amused glance. "I was with you when you bought those jeans, remember? You're a size forty-two."

Ugh! She hated European sizing. She stood beside him while he purchased their entry and noted that a good number of people passed through the turnstiles with just a flash of a blue card.

"They don't have to pay?"

"They have a medical pass," he explained as he fastened a band around her wrist. "The government operates all spas in Hungary. They're actually part of our health care system. Doctors regularly send patients here for massage or hot soaks or swimming laps."

Impressed but still a little doubtful, Natalie accompanied him into a gloriously ornate lobby, then to a seemingly mile-long hall with windows offering an unimpeded view of a sparkling swimming pool. Swimmers of all ages, shapes and sizes floated, dog-paddled or cut through the water with serious strokes.

"Here's where we temporarily part ways," Dom told her, extracting one of the towels from her tote. "The men's changing area is on the right, the women's on the left. Just show the attendant your wristband and she'll fix you up with a suit. Then hold the band up to the electronic pad and it'll assign you a changing cabin and locker. Once you've changed, flash the band again to enter the thermal baths. I'll meet you there."

That sounded simple enough—until Natalie walked through the entrance to the women's area. It was huge, with marble everywhere, stairs leading up and down, and seemingly endless rows of massage rooms, saunas, showers and changing rooms. A friendly local helped her locate the alcove containing the suit rental desk.

She still harbored distinct doubts about shimmying into a used bathing suit. But when she slid the chit Dom had given her across the desk, the attendant returned with a sealed package containing what looked like a brand-new one-piece. She held her wristband up to the electronic pad as Dom had instructed and got the number of a changing room. Faced with long, daunting rows of cubicles, she had to ask another local for help locating hers. Once they'd found it, the smiling woman took Natalie's wrist and aimed the band at the electronic lock.

"Here, here. Like this."

The door popped open, and her helpful guide added further instructions.

"It locks behind you, yes? You leave your clothes and towels in the cabin, then go through to the thermal pool."

"Thank you."

"Szívesen."

The room was larger than Natalie had expected, with a bench running along one wall and a locker for her clothes and tote. She was still leery of the rented bathing suit but a close inspection showed it to be clean and fresh-smelling.

And at least one size too small!

Cut high on the thighs and low in the front, the sleek black Spandex revealed far more skin than Natalie wanted to display. She tried yanking up the neck but that only pulled the Spandex into an all-too-suggestive V at her crotch. She tugged it down again, determined not to give Dom a peep show.

Not that he would object. The man was nothing if not appreciative of the opposite sex. Kiss Kiss Arabella and lushly endowed Lisel were proof of that. And, Natalie now remembered, his sister Zia and Sarah's sister Gina had both joked about how women fell all over him. And why not? With that sexy grin and too-handsome face, Dominic St. Sebastian could have his pick of...

She froze, her fingers still tugging at the bottom of the suit, as another handsome face flashed into her mind.

Oh, God!

She dropped onto the bench. Blood drained from her heart and gathered like a cold, dead pool in her belly.

Oh God, oh God, oh God!

Wrapping her arms around her middle, she rocked back and forth on the bench. She remembered now the "traumatic" event she'd tried to desperately to suppress. The ugly incident that had caused her to lose her sense of self.

How could she have forgotten for a day—an hour!— the vicious truth she'd kept buried for more than three years? Tears stung her eyes, raked her throat. Furiously, she fought them back. She'd cried all the tears she had in her three years ago. She was damned if she'd shed any more for the bastard who destroyed her life then. And would now destroy it again, she acknowledged on a wave of despair.

How could she have let herself believe last night could lead to something more between her and Dominic St. Sebastian? When she told him about her past, he'd be so disappointed, so disgusted. She sat there, aching for what might have been, until the urge to howl like a wounded animal released its death grip on her throat. Then she got off the bench and pushed through the door at the other end of the changing room.

The temperature in the marble hall shot up as she approached the first of the thermal pools. Dom was there, waiting for her as promised. Yesterday, even this morning, she would have drooled at the sight of his tall, muscled torso sporting a scant few inches of electric-blue Speedo. Now all she could do was gulp when he got a look at her face and stiffened.

"What's wrong?"

"I...I..."

"Natalie, what is it? What's happened?"

"I have to tell you something." She threw a wild look around the busy spa. "But not here. I'll...I'll meet you at the car."

Whirling, she fled back to her changing room.

Twelve

Her mind drowning in a cesspool of memories, Natalie scrambled into her clothes and had to ask for directions several times before she emerged from the maze of saunas and massage rooms.

Dom waited at the entrance to the women's changing rooms instead of at the car. His face was tight with concern and unspoken questions when she emerged. He swept a sharp glance around the hall, as though checking to see if anyone lingered nearby or appeared to be waiting or watching for Natalie, then cut his gaze back to her.

"What happened in the changing area to turn your face so pale?"

"I remembered something."

"About Janos Lagy?"

"No." She gnawed on her lower lip. "An incident in my past. I need to tell you about it."

Something flickered in his eyes. Surprise? Caution? Wariness? It came and went so quickly she couldn't have pinned a label on it even if her thoughts weren't skittering all over the place.

"There's a café across the street. We can talk there."

"A café? I don't think… I don't know…"

"We haven't eaten since breakfast. Whatever you have to tell me will go down easier with a bowl of goulash."

Natalie knew nothing could make it go down easier,

but she accompanied him out of the hotel and into the fall dusk. Lights had begun to glow on the Pest side of the Danube. She barely registered the glorious panorama of gold and indigo as Dom took her arm and steered her to the brightly lit café.

Soon—too soon for her mounting dread—they were enclosed in a high-backed booth that afforded both privacy and an unimpeded view of the illuminated majesty across the river. Dom ordered and signaled for her to wait until the server had brought them both coffee and a basket of thick black bread. He cut Natalie's coffee with a generous helping of milk to suit her American taste buds, then nudged the cup across the table.

"Take a drink, take a breath and tell me what has you so upset."

She complied with the first two instructions but couldn't find a way to broach the third. She stirred more milk into her coffee, fiddled with her spoon, gnawed on her lower lip again.

"Natalie. Tell me."

Her eyes lifted to his. "The scum you hunt down? The thieves and con artists and other criminals?" Misery choked her voice. "I'm one of them."

She'd dreaded his reaction. Anticipated his disgust or icy withdrawal. The fact that he didn't even blink at the anguished confession threw her off for a moment. But only a moment.

"Oh, my God! You know?" Shame coursed through her, followed almost immediately by a scorching realization. "Of course you do! You've known all along, haven't you?"

"Not all along, and not the details." His calm, even tone countered the near hysteria in hers. "Only that you were arrested, the charges were later dropped and the record wiped clean."

Her laugh was short and bitter. "Not clean enough, apparently."

The server arrived then with their goulash. The brief interruption didn't give her nearly enough time to swallow the fact that Dom had been privy to her deepest, darkest, most mortifying secret. The server departed, but the steaming soup sat untouched while Natalie related the rest of her sorry tale.

"I'm not sure how much you know about me, but before Sarah hired me I worked for the State of Illinois. Specifically, for the state's Civil Service Board. I was part of an ongoing project to digitize more than a hundred years' worth of paper files and merge them with current electronic records. I enjoyed the work. It was such a challenge putting all those old records into a sortable database."

She really *had* loved her job, she remembered as she plucked a slice of coarse black bread from the basket and played with it. Not just the digitizing and merging and sorting, but the picture those old personnel records painted of previous generations. Their work ethic, their frugal saving habits, their large numbers of dependents and generous contributions to church and charity. For someone like Natalie with no parents or grandparents or any known family, these glimpses into the quintessential American working family were fascinating.

"Then," she said with a long, slow, thoroughly disgusted sigh, "I fell in love."

She tore a thick piece off the bread, squeezed it into a wad, rolled it around and around between her fingers.

"He was so good-looking," she said miserably. "Tall, athletic, blue-eyed, always smiling."

"Always smiling? Sounds like a jerk."

Her lips twisted. "I was the jerk. I bought his line about wanting to settle down and start a family. Actually started weaving fantasies about a nursery, a minivan with car seats, the whole baby scene. I should've known I wasn't the type to interest someone as smooth and sophisticated as Jason DeWitt for longer than it took for him to hack into my computer."

Dom reached out and put his palm over the fingers still nervously rolling the bread. His grip was strong and warm, his eyes glinting with undisguised anger.

"We'll discuss what type you are later. Right now, I can pretty well guess what came next. Mr. Smooth used your computer to access state records and mine thousands of addresses, dates of birth and social security numbers."

"Try hundreds of thousands."

"Then he sold them, right? I'm guessing to the Russians, although the marketplace is pretty well wide-open these days. And when the crap hit the fan, the feds tracked the breach to you."

"He hadn't sold them yet. They caught him with his hand still in my cookie jar."

Shame and misery engulfed her again. Tears burned as the images from that horrible day played through her head.

"Oh, Dom, it was so awful! The police came to my office! Said they'd been after Jason—the man I *knew* as Jason DeWitt—for over a year. They'd decoded his electronic signature and knew he'd hacked into several major databases. They'd finally penetrated his shields and not only pinpointed his exact location, they kicked in the door to my apartment and nailed him in the act. Then they charged me with being an accomplice to unauthorized access to public records with intent to commit fraud. They arrested me right there in front of all my coworkers and... and..."

She had to stop and gulp back the stinging tears. "Then they hauled me downtown in handcuffs."

"At which point they discovered you weren't a party to the hacking and released you."

Dom's unquestioned acceptance of her innocence should have soothed her raw nerves. Instead, it made it even tougher to finish the sordid tale.

"Not quite."

Writhing inside, she tried to pull her hand away but he kept it caged.

"Jason tried to convince the police it was all my idea. He said I'd teased and taunted him with sex. That would have been laughable," she said, heat surging into her cheeks, "if the police hadn't found a closet full of crotch-high leather skirts, low-cut blouses and peek-a-boo lingerie. Jason kept pestering me to wear that kind of…of slut stuff when we went out. It was enough to make the investigators wring me inside out before they finally released me."

Dom played his thumb over the back of her hand and fought to keep his fury in check. It wasn't enough that the hacker had played on Natalie's lonely childhood and craving for a family. The bastard had also cajoled her into decking herself out like a whore. No wonder she'd swung to the opposite extreme and started dressing like a refugee from a war zone.

Even worse, she'd had no one to turn to for help during what had to be one of the most humiliating moments of her life. No parents to rush downtown and bail her out. No sister to descend like an avenging angel, as Zia would have done. No brother to pulverize the man who'd set her up.

She wasn't alone now, though. Nor would she be alone in the future. Not as long as Dominic had a say in the matter. The absolute certainty of that settled around his heart like a glove as he quietly prompted her to continue.

"What did you do then?"

"I hired a lawyer and got the arrest expunged. Or so I thought," she amended with a frown. "Then I had the lawyer negotiate a deal with my boss. Since the state records hadn't actually been compromised, I said I would quietly disappear if he agreed that my employment record would contain no reference to the whole sorry mess. After some weeks of wrangling with the state attorney general's office, I packed up and left town. I worked at odd jobs for a while until…"

"Until you went to work for Sarah," he finished when she didn't.

Guilt flooded her face. "I didn't lie to her, Dom. I filled out my employment history truthfully. I knew she would check my references, knew my chances were iffy at best. But my former boss stuck to his end of the deal, and my performance reports before…before that big mess were so glowing and complimentary that Sarah hired me after only one interview."

She turned away, shamefaced.

"I know you think I should have told her. I wanted to. I really did. And I intended to. I just thought…maybe if I tracked down the Canaletto first…helped return it to its rightful owner…Sarah and Dev and the duchess would know I wasn't a thief."

"You're not a thief. Natalie, look at me. You're not a thief or a con artist or a criminal. Trust me, I've been around the breed enough to know. Now I have two questions for you before we eat the soup that's been sitting here for so long."

"Only two?"

Her voice was wobbly, her eyes still tear-bright and drenched with a humiliation that made Dom vow to pulverize the scum who'd put it there.

"Where is this Jason character now?"

"Serving five to ten at the Danville Correctional Facility."

"Well, that takes him off my hit list. For now."

An almost smile worked through her embarrassment. "What's question two?"

"How long are you going to keep mashing that piece of bread?"

She blinked and looked down in surprise at the pulpy glob squishing through her fingers.

"Here." He passed her a napkin. "Eat your soup, *drágám*. Then we'll go home and get back to work on finding your painting."

Home. The word reverberated in Natalie's mind when Dom opened the door to the loft and Duke treated them to an ecstatic welcome. She clung to the sound of it, the thought of it, like a lifeline while man and dog took a quick trip downstairs and she went to unpack the roller suitcase still propped next to the wardrobe.

Her toiletries went into the bathroom, her underwear onto the corner of a shelf in the wardrobe. When she lifted the neatly folded blouses, her mouth twisted.

Natalie knew she'd never been a Princess Kate. She wasn't tall or glamorous or as poised as a supermodel. But she'd possessed her own sense of style. She'd preferred a layered look, she now remembered. Mostly slim slacks or jeans with belted tunics or cardigans over tanks...until Jason.

He'd wanted sexier, flashier. She cringed, remembering how she'd suppressed her inner qualms and let him talk her into those thigh-hugging skirts and lace-up bustiers. She'd burned them. The leather skirts, the bustiers, the stilettos and boob tubes and garter belts and push-up bras. Carted the whole lot down to the incinerator in her building, along with every other item in her apartment that carried even a whiff of Jason's scent or a faint trace of his imprint.

Then she'd gone out and purchased an entire new wardrobe of maiden aunt blouses and shapeless linen dresses. She'd also stopped using makeup and began scraping her hair back in a bun. She'd even resorted to wearing glasses she didn't need. Paying penance, she now realized, for her sins.

She was still staring at the folded blouses when Dom and the hound returned. When he saw what she was holding, he dropped the dog's lead on the kitchen counter and crossed the room.

"You don't need these anymore." He took the blouses and dumped them back in the case. "You don't need any of this."

When he zipped the case and propped it next to the wardrobe again, Natalie experienced a heady sense of freedom. As though she'd just shed an outer skin that'd felt as unnatural and uncomfortable as the one she'd tried to squeeze into for Jason.

Buoyed by the feeling, she flashed Dom a smile. "If you don't want me to continue raiding your closet, you'll have to take me shopping again."

"You're welcome to wear anything of mine you wish. Although," he confessed with a quick grin, "I must admit I prefer when you wear nothing at all."

The need that splintered through her was swift and clean and joyous. The shame she'd tried to bury for three long years was still there, just below the surface. She suspected traces of it would linger there for a long while. But for now, for this moment, she could give herself completely to Dom and her aching hunger for his touch.

She looped her arms around his neck and let the smile in his eyes begin healing the scars. "I must admit I prefer you that way, too."

"Then I suggest we both shed some clothes."

They made it to the bed. Barely. A stern command prevented Duke from jumping in with them, but Natalie had to force herself not to look at the hound's reproachful face until Dom's mouth and teeth and busy, busy hands made her forget everything but him.

She was boneless with pleasure and half-asleep when he tucked her into the curve of his body and murmured something in Hungarian.

"What does that mean?"

"Sleep well, my darling."

Her heart tripped, but she didn't ask him to expand on that interesting translation. She settled for snuggling closer to his warmth and drifting into a deep, dreamless sleep.

Natalie woke the next morning to the sound of hammering. She pried one eye open and listened for several moments before realizing that was rain pounding against the roof. Burrowing deeper under the featherbed, she resurfaced again only when an amused voice sounded just over her shoulder.

"The dog and I are going for our run. Coffee's on the stove when you're ready for it."

She half rolled over. "You're going out in the rain?"

"That's one of the penalties of being adopted by a racing hound. He needs regular exercise whatever the weather. We both do, actually."

Natalie grunted, profoundly thankful that she wasn't invited to participate in this morning ritual.

"I'll bring back apple pancakes for breakfast," Dom advised as he and the joyously prancing Agár headed for the door. "Then we'll need to leave for the appointments at the embassy and the Tax and Customs Administration."

"And shopping," Natalie called to his back. "I need to shop!"

The prospect of replenishing her wardrobe with bright colors and soft textures erased any further desire to burrow. By the time Dom and Duke returned she'd showered and dressed in her one pair of jeans and tank top. She'd also made the bed, fussed with the folds in the drapes and dust-mopped the loft's wood-plank floors.

Her welcome smile slipped a little when the runners tracked wet foot- and paw-prints across the gleaming floors. She had to laugh, though, and hold up her hands against a flying spray when the hound planted all four paws and shook from his nose to his tail.

She and Dom feasted on the pancakes that he'd somehow protected from the rain. Then he, too, got ready for the morning's appointments. He emerged from the bathroom showered and shaved and looking too scrumptious for words in jeans and a cable-knit fisherman's sweater.

"You'd better bring the Canaletto file," he advised.

"I have it," she said, patting her briefcase. "I made copies of the key documents, just in case."

"Good." He held up the jacket she'd pretty much claimed as her own. "Now put this on and we'll go."

Natalie was glad of its warmth when they went down to the car. The rain had lessened to a misty drizzle but the damp chill carried a bite. Not even the gray weather could obscure the castle ramparts, though, as Dom negotiated the curving streets of Castle Hill and joined the stream of traffic flowing across Chain Bridge.

The US Embassy was housed in what had once been an elegant turn-of-the century palazzo facing a lush park. High metal fencing and concrete blocks had turned it into a modern-day fortress and long lines waited to go through the security checkpoint. As Dom steered Natalie to a side entrance with a much shorter line, she noted a bronze plaque with a raised relief religious figure.

"Who's that?"

"Cardinal József Mindszenty, one of the heroes of modern Hungary. The communists tortured and imprisoned him for speaking out against their brutal regime. He got a temporary reprieve during the 1956 Revolution, but when the Soviets crushed the uprising, the US Embassy granted him political asylum. He remained here for more than fifteen years.

"Fifteen *years*?"

"Cardinal Mindszenty is one of the reasons Hungary and the United States enjoy such close ties today."

Dom's Interpol credentials got them into the consular offices through the side entrance. After passing through security and X-ray screening, they arrived at their appointment right on time

Replacing Natalie's lost passport took less than a half hour. She produced the copy of her driver's license Dom's contact had procured and the forms she'd already completed. After signing the form in front of a consular officer and having it witnessed by another official, the computer spit out a copy of her passport's data page.

She winced at the photo, taken when she'd renewed her passport just over a year ago, but she thanked the official and slipped the passport into her tote with an odd, unsettled feeling. She should have been relieved to have both her memory and her identity back. She could leave Hungary now. Go home to the States, or anywhere else her research took her. How stupid was she for wishing this passport business had taken weeks instead of minutes?

Their second appointment didn't go as quickly or as well. Dom's Interpol credentials seemed to have a negative effect on the two uniformed officers they met with at the NTCA. One was a spare, thirtysomething woman who introduced herself as Patrícia Czernek, the other a graying older man who greeted Natalie with a polite nod before engaging Dom in a spirited dialogue. It didn't take a genius or a working knowledge of Hungarian to figure out they were having a bit of a turf war. Natalie kept out of the line of fire until the female half of the team picked up the phone and made a call that appeared to settle the matter.

With a speaking glance at her partner, Officer Czernek turned to Natalie. "So Ms. Clark, we understand from Special Agent St. Sebastian that you may have knowledge of a missing painting by a Venetian master. One taken from Karlenburgh Castle during the 1956 Uprising. Will you tell us, please, how you came by this knowledge?"

"Certainly."

Extracting the Canaletto file, she passed each of the officers a copy of the chronology she'd run earlier. "This summarizes my research, step-by-step. As you can see, it began three months ago with a computer search."

The NTCA officers flipped through the four-sheet printout and exchanged looks. Dom merely smiled.

"If you'll turn to page three, line thirty-seven," Natalie continued briskly, "you'll see that I did a search of recently declassified documents from the Soviet era relating to art treasures owned by the state and found an inventory of items removed from Karlenburgh Castle. The inventory listed more than two dozen near priceless works of art, but not the Canaletto. Yet I knew from previous discussions with Grand Duchess Charlotte that the painting *was* hanging in the Red Salon the day the Soviets came to destroy the castle."

She walked them through her search step-by-step. Her decision to drive down from Vienna to interview local residents. Her stop at the ruins and meeting with Friedrich Müller. His reference to an individual who'd inquired previously at the Red Salon.

"Janos Lagy," the older of the two officers murmured. He skimmed down several lines and looked up quickly. "You spoke with him? You spoke with Lagy about this painting?"

"I did."

"And arranged to meet with him on a riverboat?"

"That was his idea, not mine. Unfortunately, he didn't show."

"Do you have a recording of this conversation?" Officer Czernek asked hopefully. "On your cell phone, perhaps?"

"I lost my purse and phone when I went overboard."

"Yes, Special Agent St. Sebastian told us about your accident." A frown etched between her brows. "We also reviewed a copy of the incident report from the metropolitan police. It's very strange that no one saw you fall from the boat or raised an alarm."

"I was at the back of the ship and not feeling very well. Also, this happened in the middle of the week. There weren't many other passengers aboard."

"Still…"

She and her partner engaged in a brief exchange.

"We, too, have a file," she said, turning back to Natalie. "Would you be so kind as to look at some pictures and tell me if you recognize any of the people in them?"

She produced a thin folder and slid out three eight-by-tens. One showed a lone figure in a business suit and tie. The second picture was of the same individual in a tux and smiling down at the svelte beauty on his arm. In the third, he strolled along a city street wearing an overcoat and smart fedora.

"Do you recognize that man?" Czernek asked, her gaze intent on Natalie.

She scrutinized the lean features again. The confident smile, the dark eyes and fringe of brown hair around a head going bald on top. She'd never seen him before. She was sure of it.

"No, I don't recognize him. Is it Lagy?"

The police officer nodded and blew out an obviously disappointed breath. When she reached over to gather the pictures, Natalie had to battle her own crushing disappointment. Lagy's link to the Canaletto had been tenuous at best but she'd followed thinner threads. Suddenly, she frowned and took another look at the street shot.

"Him!" She stabbed a finger at a figure trailing a little way behind Lagy. "I recognize this man. He was on the boat."

"Are you sure?"

"Very sure. When I got sick, he asked if he could help but I waved him away. I didn't want to puke all over his shoes." She looked up eagerly. "Do you know who he is?"

"He's Janos Lagy's bodyguard."

The air in the small office suddenly simmered with rigidly suppressed excitement. Natalie looked from Czernek to her partner to Dom and back again. All of them, apparently, knew something she didn't.

"Clue me in," she demanded. "What have you got on Janos Lagy?"

The officer hesitated. A cop's natural instinct to hold her cards close to her chest, Natalie guessed. Tough! She wasn't leaving the NTCA until she got some answers.

"Look," she said mutinously, "I've chased all over Europe tracking the Canaletto. I've spent weeks digging through musty records. I whacked my head and took an unplanned swim in the Danube. I didn't know who I was for almost a week. So I think I deserve an answer. What's the story on Lagy?"

After another brief pause, Czernek relented. "We've had him under surveillance for some time now. We suspect he's been trafficking in stolen art and have unsubstantiated reports of a private collection kept in a secret vault in his home."

"You're kidding!"

"No, I am not. Unfortunately, we haven't been able to gather enough evidence to convince a judge to issue a search warrant." Patrícia Czernek's lips parted in a knife blade of a smile. "Based on what you've told us, we may be able to get that warrant."

Thirteen

After all she'd done, all she'd been through, Natalie considered it a complete and total bummer that she was forced to sit on the sidelines during the final phase of the hunt that had consumed her for so many weeks.

The task force gathered early the morning after Natalie had ID'd the bodyguard. As tenuous as that connection was to Lagy and the missing Canaletto, when combined with other evidence NCTA had compiled on the banker, it proved sufficient for a judge to grant a search warrant. Dom left the loft before dawn to join the team that would hit the banker's villa on the outskirts of Budapest. Natalie was left behind with nothing to do but walk the hound, make another excursion to the butcher shop, scrub the shower stall, dust-mop the floors again and pace.

"This is the pits," she complained to the hound as the morning dragged by.

The Agár cocked his head but didn't look particularly sympathetic.

"Okay, okay! It's true I don't have any official standing that could have allowed them to include me in the task force. And I guess I don't really want to see anyone hauled off in handcuffs. That would cut a little too close to the bone," she admitted with a grimace. "Still," she grumbled, shooting another glance at the kitchen clock, "you'd think certain people would find a way to let me know what's happening."

Dominic couldn't contact her directly. She knew that. Natalie's phone was at the bottom of the Danube and the loft didn't have a landline. He could've called his downstairs neighbors, though, and asked Katya or her father to relay a message.

Or not. There was probably some rule or protocol that prohibited disseminating information about an ongoing investigation to civilians.

"That better not include me."

The bad-tempered comment produced a nervous whine from the hound. Natalie stooped to scratch behind his ear.

"Sorry, Duke'ums. I'm just a little annoyed with your alter ego."

Annoyed and increasingly worried as morning crawled toward noon, then into the afternoon, she was seriously contemplating going downstairs to ask Katya if she could use her phone when she heard the heavy tread of footsteps on the outside stairs.

"Finally!"

She rushed to the door, startling the dog into a round of excited barking. One look at Dom's mile-wide grin sent all her nasty recriminations back down her throat. She could only laugh when he caught her by the waist and swung her in wide circles. The hound, of course, went nuts. Natalie had to call a halt before they all tripped over each other and tumbled down five flights of stairs.

"Dom, stop! You're making me dizzy."

He complied with a smooth move that shifted her from mostly vertical to horizontal. Still wearing a cheek-splitting grin, he carried her over the threshold and kicked the door shut as soon as the three of them were inside.

"I assume you got your man," she said.

"You assume right. Hold on."

He opened the fridge and dipped her almost vertical again. Squealing, she locked her arms around his neck while he retrieved two frosty bottles from the bottom shelf, then carried her to the sofa. He sank onto the cushions with Natalie in his lap and thumped his boots up on the coffee table.

She managed to keep from pelting him with questions while he offered her one of the dew-streaked bottles of pilsner. When she shook her head, he popped the cap and tilted his head. She watched, fascinated, as he downed half the contents in long, thirsty swallows. He hadn't had time to shave before he'd left. The beginnings of a beard shadowed his cheeks and chin. And his knuckles, she noted with a small gasp, had acquired a nasty set of scrapes and bruises.

"What happened to your knuckles?"

"Lagy's bodyguard ran into them." Something dark and dangerous glinted in his eyes. "Several times."

"What? Why?"

"We had a private discussion about your swim in the Danube. He disavowed any responsibility for it, of course, but I didn't like the way his lip curled when he did."

She gaped at him, her jaw sagging. She'd been alone so long. And so sickened by the way Jason had tried to pin the blame for his illegal activities on her. The idea that Dom had set himself up as her protector and avenger cut deep into her heart. Before she could articulate the chaotic emotions those bruised knuckles roused, however, the hound almost climbed into her lap.

She held him off, but it took some effort. "You'd better give him some of your beer before he grabs the bottle out of your hand, and tell me the rest of the story!"

He tipped the bottle toward the Agár's eager jaws. Natalie barely registered an inward cringe as pale gold lager slopped in all directions. Duke dropped the empty bottle on the floor and was scooting it across the oak planks to extract the last drops when Dom launched into a detailed account.

"We hit the villa before Lagy had left for the bank. When Czernek showed him the search warrant, he wouldn't let us proceed until his high-priced lawyer arrived on the scene."

"Did Lagy recognize you?"

"Oh, yeah. He made some crack about the newspaper stories, but I could tell the fact that a St. Sebastian had showed up at his door with an armed squad made him nervous. Especially when I flashed my Interpol credentials."

"Then what happened?"

"We cooled our heels until his lawyer showed up. Bastard had the nerve to play lord of the manor and offer us all coffee."

"Which you accepted," she guessed, all too mindful of the Hungarian passion for the brew.

"Which we accepted," he confirmed. "By the time his lawyer arrived, though, we'd all had our fill of acting polite. His attorney tried to posture and bluff, but folded like an accordion when Czernek waved the search warrant under his nose. Apparently he'd gotten crosswise of this particular judge before and knew he couldn't fast-talk his client out of this one. Then," Dom said with savage satisfaction, "we tore the villa apart. Imagine our surprise when infrared imaging detected a vault hidden behind a false wall in Lagy's study."

When he paused to pop the cap on the second bottle, Natalie groaned in sheer frustration.

"Don't you dare drink that before you tell me what was in the vault!"

"See for yourself." Shifting her on his lap, he jammed a hand in the pocket of his jeans and extracted a folded printout. "That's just a preliminary inventory. Each piece has to be examined and authenticated by a team of experts."

Her hands shaking with excitement, Natalie unfolded the printout and skimmed the fourteen entries.

"Omigod!"

The list read like a who's who of the art world. Edgar Degas. Josef Grassi. Thomas Gainsborough. And there, close to the bottom, Giovanni Canaletto.

"Did you see the Canaletto?" she asked breathlessly. "Is it the one from Karlenburgh Castle?"

"Looked like it to me."

"I can't believe it!"

"Lagy couldn't, either, when Czernek called for a team to crate up his precious paintings and take them in evidence."

She skimmed the list again, stunned by its variety and richness. "How incredible that he managed to amass such an extensive collection. It must be worth hundreds of millions."

"He may have acquired some of it through legitimate channels. As for the rest…" Dom's jaw hardened. "I'm guessing he inherited many of those paintings from his grandfather. Karlenburgh Castle wasn't the only residence destroyed in retribution for their owners' participation in the '56 Uprising. *Mladshij Lejtenant* Lagy's company of sappers would have been only too eager help take them down. God knows how many treasures the bastards managed to appropriate for themselves in the process."

Natalie slumped against his chest and devoured the brief descriptions of the paintings removed from Lagy's villa. Several she recognized immediately from Interpol's database of lost or stolen art. Others she would need more detail on before she could be sure.

"This," she said, excitement still singing through her veins, "is going make a fantastic final chapter in Sarah's book. Her editors will eat up the personal angle. A painting purchased for a young duchess, then lost for decades. The hunt by the duchess's granddaughter for the missing masterpiece. The raid that recovered it, which just happened to include the current Grand Duke."

"Let's not forget the part you played in the drama."

"I'm just the research assistant. You St. Sebastians are the star players."

"You're not 'just' anything, Natushka."

To emphasize the point, he tugged on her hair and tilted her head back for a long, hard kiss. Neither of them held back, taking and giving in both a welcome release of tension and celebration.

Natalie was riding high when Dom raised his head. "I can't wait to tell Sarah about this. And the duchess! When do you think her painting will be returned to her?"

"I have no idea. They'll have to authenticate it first, then trace the provenance. If Lagy can prove he purchased it or any of these paintings in good faith from a gallery or another collector, the process could take weeks or months."

"Or longer," she said, scrunching her nose. "Can't you exert some royal influence and hurry the process along?"

"Impatient little thing, aren't you?"

"And then some!" She scooted off his lap and onto the cushion next to him. "Let's contact Sarah via FaceTime. I want to see her reaction when we tell her."

They caught Sarah in midair aboard Dev's private jet. The moment Dom made the connection, her employer fired an anxious query.

"How's Natalie? Has her memory returned?"

"It has."

"Thank God! Where is she now?"

"She's here, with me. Hang on."

He angled the phone to capture Natalie's eager face. "Hello, Sarah."

"Oh, Natalie, we've been so worried. Are you really okay?"

"Better than okay. We've located the Canaletto!"

"What?" Sarah whipped her head to one side. "Dev, you're not going to believe this! Natalie's tracked down Grandmama's Canaletto."

"I didn't do it alone," Natalie protested, aiming a quick smile at Dom. "It was a team effort."

When she glanced back at the screen, Sarah's brows had inched up. "Well," she said after a small pause, "if I was going to team with anyone other than my husband, Dominic would certainly top my list."

A telltale heat rushed into Natalie's cheeks but she didn't respond to the curiosity simmering just below the surface of her employer's reply. Mostly because she wasn't really sure how to define her "teaming" with Dom, much less predict how long it would last. But she couldn't hold back a cheek-to-cheek grin as she related the events of the past few days. Sarah's eyes grew wider with the telling, and at the end of the recital she echoed Natalie's earlier sentiments.

"This is all so incredible. I can't wait to tell Grandmama the Canaletto's been recovered."

Dom leaned over Natalie's shoulder to issue the same warning he had earlier. "They'll have to assemble a team of experts to authenticate each painting and validate its provenance. That could take several months or more."

Dev's face crowded next to his wife's on the small screen. "We'll see what we can do to expedite the process, at least as far as the Canaletto is concerned."

"And I'll ask Gina to get Jack involved," Sarah volunteered. "He can apply some subtle pressure through diplomatic channels."

"I also suggested to the Grand Duke here that he should exercise a little royal muscle," Natalie put in.

"Good for you. With all three of our guys weighing in, I'm sure we can shake Grandmama's painting loose without too long a delay."

The reference to "our" guys deepened the heat in Natalie's cheeks. She floundered for a moment, but before she could think of an appropriate response to the possessive pronoun, Sarah had already jumped ahead.

"We need to update the chapter on the Canaletto, Nat. And if we put our noses to the grindstone, we ought to be able to finish the final draft of the book in two or three weeks. When can you fly back to L.A.?"

"I, uh…"

"Scratch that. Instead of going straight home, let's rendezvous in New York. I'd like you to personally brief my editor. I know she'll want to take advantage of the publicity all this is going to generate. We can fly to L.A. from there."

She could hardly say no. Sarah St. Sebastian Hunter had offered her the job of a lifetime. Not only did Natalie love the work, she appreciated the generous salary and fringe benefits that came with it. She owed her boss loyalty and total dedication until her book hit the shelves.

"No problem. I can meet you in New York whenever it works for you."

"I'll call my editor as soon as we hang up. I'll try to arrange something on Thursday or Friday. Did you get a replacement passport? Great. You should probably fly home tomorrow, then. I'll have a ticket waiting for you at the airport."

She disconnected with a promise to call back as soon as she'd nailed down the time and place of the meeting. Dominic tossed his phone on the coffee table and turned to Natalie.

She couldn't quite meet his eyes. She felt as though

she'd just dropped down an elevator shaft. Mere moments ago she'd been riding a dizzying high. In a few short seconds, she'd plunged back into cold, hard reality. She had a job, responsibilities, a life back in the States, such as it was. And neither she nor Dom had discussed any alternative. Still, the prospect of leaving Hungary drilled a hole in her heart.

"Sarah's been so good to me," she said, breaking the small silence. "I need to help put the final touches on her book."

"Of course you do. I, too, must go back to work. I've been away from it too long."

She plucked at the hem of her borrowed shirt. She should probably ask Dom to take her on a quick shopping run. She could hardly show up for a meeting with Sarah's editor in jeans and a tank top, much less a man's soccer shirt. Yet she hated to spend her last hours in Budapest cruising boutiques.

She tried to hide her misery at the thought of leaving, but Dom had to see it when he curled a knuckle under her chin and tipped her face to his.

"Perhaps this is for the best, *drágám*. You've had so much thrown at you in such a short time. The dive into the Danube. The memory loss. Me," he said with a crooked grin. "You need to step back and take a breath."

"You're probably right," she mumbled.

"I know I am. And when you've helped Sarah put her book to bed, you and I will decide where we go from there, yes?"

She wanted to believe him. Ached all over with the need to throw herself into his arms and make him *swear* this wasn't the end. Unfortunately, all she could think of was Kiss Kiss Arabella's outrageously expensive panties and Lovely Lisel's effusive greeting and Gina's laughing comments about her studly cousin and…

Dominic cut into those lowering thoughts by tugging her up and off the sofa with him. "So! Since this is your last night in Budapest for a while at least, we should make it one to remember."

For a while at least. Natalie clung to the promise of that small phrase as Dom scooped up his phone and stuffed it in his jeans pocket. Taking time only to pull on the red-and-black soccer shirt with its distinctive logo on the sleeve, he insisted she throw on the jacket she'd pretty much claimed as her own before hustling her to the door.

"Where are we going?"

"My very favorite place in all the city."

Since the city boasted spectacular architecture, a world-class opera house, soaring cathedrals, palatial spas and a moonlit, romantic castle perched high on its own hill, Natalie couldn't begin to guess which was Dom's favorite spot. She certainly wouldn't have picked the café/bar he ushered her into on the Pest side of the river. It was tiny, just one odd-shaped room, and noisy and crammed with men decked out in red-and-black-striped shirts. Most were around Dom's age, although Natalie saw a sprinkling of both freckles and gray hair among the men. Many stood with arms looped over the shoulders or around the waists of laughing, chatting women.

They were greeted with hearty welcomes and backslaps and more than one joking "His Grace" or "Grand Duke." Dom made so many introductions Natalie didn't even try to keep names and faces matched. As the beer flowed and his friends graciously switched to English to include her in the lively conversation, she learned she would have a ringside seat—via satellite and high-definition TV—at the World Cup European playoffs. Hungary's team had been eliminated in the quarterfinals, much to the disgust of everyone in the bar, but they'd grudgingly shifted their allegiance to former rival Slovakia.

With such a large crowd and such limited seating, Natalie watched the game, nestled on Dom's lap. Hoots and boos and foot-stomping thundered after every contested call. Cheers and ear-splitting whistles exploded when Slovakia scored halfway through the first quarter. Or was it the first half? Third? Natalie had no clue.

She was deafened by the noise, jammed knee to knee with strangers, breathing in the tang of beer and healthy male sweat, and she loved every minute of it! The noise, the excitement, the color, the casually possessive arm Dom hooked around her waist. She filed away every sensory impression, every scent and sound and vivid visual image, so she could retrieve them later. When she was back in New York or L.A. or wherever she landed after Sarah's book hit the shelves.

She refused to dwell on the uncertain future during the down-to-the-wire game. Nor while she and Dom took the hound for a romp through the park at the base of the castle. Not even when they returned to the loft and he hooked his arms around her waist as she stood in front of the wall of windows, drinking in her last sight of the Parliament's floodlit dome and spires across the river.

"It's so beautiful," she murmured.

"Like you," he said, nuzzling her ear.

"Ha! Not hardly."

"You don't see what I see."

He turned her, keeping her in the circle of his arms, and cradled her hips against his. His touch was featherlight as he stroked her cheek.

"Your skin is so soft, so smooth. And your eyes reflect your inner self. So intelligent, so brave even when you were so frightened that you would never regain your memory."

"Terrified" was closer to the mark, but she wasn't about to interrupt this interesting inventory.

Smiling, he threaded his fingers through her hair.

"I love how this goes golden-brown in the sunlight. Like thick, rich honey. It's true, your chin hints at a bit of a stubborn streak but your lips… Ah, Natushka, your lips. Have you any idea what that little pout of yours does to me?"

"Children pout," she protested. "Sultry beauties with collagen lips pout. I merely express…"

"Disapproval," he interjected, nipping at her lower lip. "Disdain. Disgust. All of which I saw in your face the first time we met. I wondered then whether I could make these same lips quiver with delight and whisper my name."

The nipping kisses achieved the first of his stated goals. Pleasure rippled across the surface of Natalie's skin even as Dom's husky murmur sent up a warning flag. She'd represented a challenge. She'd sensed that from the beginning. She remembered, too, how his sister and cousins had teased him about his many conquests. But now? Was the slow heat he stirred in her belly, the aching need in her chest, merely the by-product of a skilled seduction? Had she tumbled into love with the wrong man again?

She knew the answer before the question even half formed. Dominic St. Sebastian was most definitely the right man. The *only* man she wanted in her heart. In her life. She couldn't tell him, though. Her one and only previous foray into this love business had left her with too much baggage. Too many doubts and insecurities. And she was leaving in the morning. That more than anything else blocked the words she ached to say.

It didn't keep her from cradling his face in her palms while she kissed him long and hard. Or undressing him slowly, savoring every taut muscle, every hollow and hard plane of his body. Or groaning his name when he drove them both to a shattering climax.

Fourteen

Natalie couldn't classify the next five weeks as totally miserable.

Her first priority when she landed in New York was refurbishing her wardrobe before the meeting with Sarah and her editors. After she'd checked into her hotel she made a quick foray to Macy's. Sarah had smiled her approval at her assistant's conservative but nicely tailored navy suit and buttercup-yellow blouse.

Her smile had morphed to a wide grin when she and Natalie emerged from the meeting at Random House. Her editors were enthusiastic about how close the manuscript was to completion and anxious to get their hands on the final draft.

After a second meeting to discuss advance promo with Sarah's former boss at *Beguile* magazine, the two women flew back to California and hit the ground running. They spent most of their waking hours in Sarah's spacious, glass-walled office on the second floor of the Pacific Palisades mansion she shared with Dev. The glorious ocean view provided no distraction as they revised and edited and polished and proofed.

The final draft contained twenty-two chapters, each dedicated to a specific lost treasure. The Fabergé egg rated one chapter, the Bernini bronze another. The final chapter was devoted to the Canaletto, with space left for a photograph of the painting being restored to its rightful owner. *If* it was ever restored!

The authentication and provenance process was taking longer than any of the St. Sebastians had hoped. Several big-time insurance companies were now involved, anxious to recoup the hundreds of thousands of dollars they'd paid out over the years.

The Canaletto didn't fall into that category. It *had* been insured, as had many of the valuable objects in Karlenburgh Castle, but the policy contained exclusions for loss due to war and/or acts of God. By categorizing the 1956 Uprising as war, the insurer had wiggled out of compensating the duchess for St. Sebastian heirlooms that had either disappeared or made their way into private collections. Still, with so many conflicting claims to sort out, the team charged with verifying authenticity and rightful ownership had its hands full.

Dominic, Dev Hunter and Jack Harris had done what they could to speed the process. Dev offered to fund part of the effort. Jack helped facilitate coordination between international agencies asserting conflicting claims. Much to his disgust, Dom didn't return to undercover work. Instead, his boss at Interpol detailed him to act as their liaison to the recovery team. He grumbled about that but provided the expertise to link Lagy to several black marketeers and less reputable galleries suspected of dealing in stolen art.

He kept Sarah and Natalie apprised of the team's progress by email and texts. The personal calls came in the evenings, after Natalie had dragged back to her rented one-room condo. They'd spoken every couple of nights when she'd first returned, less frequently as both she and Dom got caught up in their separate tasks. But just the sound of his voice could make her hurt with a combination of hunger and loneliness.

The doubts crept in after she'd been home for several weeks. Dom seemed distracted when he called. After almost a month, it felt to Natalie as though he was struggling to keep any conversation going that didn't deal directly with the authentication effort.

Sarah seemed to sense her assistant's growing unease. She didn't pry, but she had a good idea what had happened between her cousin and Natalie during their time together in Budapest. She got a far clearer picture when she dropped what she thought was a casual question one rainy afternoon.

"Did Dom give you any glimmer of hope when the team might vet the Canaletto the last time he called?"

Natalie didn't look up from the dual-page layout on her computer screen. "No."

"Damn. We're supposed to fly to New York for another meeting with Random House next week. I hate to keep putting them off. Maybe you can push Dom a little next time you talk to him."

"I'm…I'm not sure when that will be."

From the corner of her eye Natalie saw Sarah's head come up. Swiveling her desk chair, she met her employer's carefully neutral look.

"Dom's been busy… The time difference… It's tough catching each other at home and…"

The facade crumbled without a hint of warning. One minute she was faking a bright smile. Two seconds later she was gulping and swearing silently that she would *not* cry.

"Oh, Natalie." Sympathy flooded Sarah's warm brown eyes. "I'm sure it's just as you say. Dom's busy, you're busy, you're continents apart…"

"And the tabloids have glommed on to him again," Natalie said with a wobbly smile.

"I know," Sarah said with a grimace. "One of these days I'll learn not to trust Alexis."

Her former boss had sworn up and down she didn't leak the story. Once it hit the press, though, *Beguile* followed almost immediately with a four-page color spread featuring Europe's sexiest single royal and his role in the recovery of stolen art worth hundreds of millions. Although the story stopped short of revealing that Dom worked for Interpol, it hinted at a dark and dangerous side to the duke. It even mentioned the Agár and obliquely suggested the hound had been trained by an elite counterterrorist strike force to sniff out potential targets. Natalie might have chuckled at that if the accompanying photo of Dom and Duke running in the park below the castle hadn't knifed right into her heart.

As a consequence, she was feeling anything but celebratory when she joined Sarah and Dev and Dev's extraordinarily efficient chief of operations, Pat Donovan, at a dinner to celebrate the book's completion. She mustered the requisite smiles and lifted her champagne flute for each toast. But she descended into a sputtering blob of incoherence when Sarah broached the possibility of a follow-on book specifically focused on Karlenburgh's colorful, seven-hundred-year history.

"Please, Natalie! Say you'll work with me on the research."

"I, uh…"

"Would you consider a one-year contract, with an option for two more? I'll double what I'm paying you now for the first year, and we can negotiate your salary for the following two."

She almost swallowed her tongue. "You're already paying me twice what the average researcher's services are worth!"

Dev leaned across the table and folded his big hand around Natalie's. "You're not just a researcher, kid. We consider you one of the family."

"Th-Thank you."

She refused to dwell on her nebulous, half-formed thoughts of actually becoming a member of their clan. Those silly hopes had faded in the past month...to the point where she wasn't sure she could remain on the fringe of Sarah's family orbit.

Her outrageously expensive dinner curdled at the thought of bumping into Dom at the launch of Sarah's book six or eight months from now. Or crossing paths with him if she returned to Hungary to research the history of the St. Sebastians. Or seeing the inevitable gossip put out by the tabloids whenever the sexy royal appeared at some gala with a glamorous female looking suspiciously like Natalie's mental image of Kissy Face Arabella.

"I'm overwhelmed by the offer," she told Sarah with a grateful smile. "Can I take a little time to think it over?"

"Of course! But think fast, okay? I'd like to brief my editors on the concept when we meet with them next week."

Before Natalie could even consider accepting Sarah's offer, she had to come clean. The next morning she burned with embarrassment as she related the whole sorry story of her arrest and abrupt departure from her position as an archivist for the State of Illinois. Sarah listened with wide eyes but flatly refused to withdraw her offer.

"Oh, Nat, I'm so sorry you got taken in by such a conniving bastard. All I can say is that he's lucky he's behind bars. He'd damned well better keep looking over his shoulder when he gets out, though. Dev and Dominic both have long memories."

Relieved by Sarah's unqualified support but racked with doubts about Dom, Natalie was still agonizing over her decision the following Tuesday, when a taxi delivered her and Sarah to the tower of steel and glass housing her publisher. Spanning half a block in downtown Manhattan, the mega-conglomerate's lobby was walled with floor-to-ceiling bookcases displaying the hundreds of books put out each month by Random House's many imprints.

It was Natalie's third time accompanying Sarah to this publishing cathedral but the display of volumes hot off the press still awed her book-lover soul. While Sarah signed them both in and waited for an escort to whisk them up to the thirty-second floor, Natalie devoured the jacket and back-cover copy of a new release detailing the events leading to World War I and its catastrophic impact on Europe. Germany and the Austro-Hungarian Empire were major players in those cataclysmic events.

Karlenburgh sat smack in the juxtaposition of those cultures and epic struggles. Natalie itched to get her hands on the book. She was scrambling for her iPhone to snap a shot of the book jacket when a shrill bark cut through the low-level hum of the busy lobby. She spun around, her jaw dropping as a brown-and-white bullet hurtled straight toward her.

"Duke!" She took two front paws hard in the stomach, staggered back, dropped to her knees. "What…? How…? Whoa! Stop, fella! Stop!"

Laughing, she twisted her head to dodge the Agár's ecstatic kisses. The sight of Dom standing at the lobby entrance, his grin as goofy as the hound's, squeezed the air from her lungs. The arms fending the dog off collapsed, Duke lunged, and they both went down.

She heard a scramble of footsteps. A frantic voice shouting for someone to call 911 or animal control or whoever. A strangled yelp as a would-be rescuer grabbed Duke's collar and yanked him off her. Sarah protesting the rough handling. Dom charging across the lobby to take control of the situation.

By the time the chaos finally subsided, he'd hauled Natalie to her feet and into his arms. "Ah, Natushka," he said, his eyes alight with laughter, "the hound and I hoped to surprise you, not cause a riot."

"Forget the riot! What are you doing in here?"

"I called Sarah's office to speak with you and was told you'd both flown to New York."

"But...but..." She couldn't get her head and her heart to work in sync. "How did you know we'd be here, at the publisher? Oh! You did your James Bond thing, didn't you?"

"I did."

"I still don't understand. You? Duke? Here?"

"We missed you."

The simple declaration shimmered like a rainbow, breathing color into the hopes and dreams that had shaded to gray.

"I planned to wait until I could bring the Canaletto," he told her, tipping his forehead to hers. "I wanted you with me when we restored the painting and all the memories it holds for the duchess. But every day, every night away from you ate at my patience. I got so restless and bad-tempered even the hound would snarl or slink away from me. The team's infuriatingly slow pace didn't help. You probably didn't notice when I called but..."

"I noticed," she drawled.

"But it all boiled down to frustration," he finished with a rueful smile. "Pure, unadulterated frustration."

She started to tell him he wasn't the only one who'd twisted and turned and tied themself up in knots but he preempted any reply by cradling her face in his palms.

"I wanted to wait before I told you that I love you, *drágám*. I wanted to give you time, let you find your feet again. I was worried, too, about the weeks and months my job would take me away. Your job, as well, if you accept the offer Dev told me about when I called to speak with you. I know your work is important to you, as mine is to me. We can work it out, yes?"

She pretty much stopped listening after the "I love you" part but caught the question in the last few words.

"Yes," she breathed with absolutely no idea what she was agreeing to. "Yes, yes, yes!"

"Then you'll take this?"

She glanced down, a laugh gurgling in her throat as Dom pinned an enameled copy of his soccer club's insignia to the lapel of her suit jacket.

"It will have to do," he told her with a look in those dark eyes that promised the love and home and family she'd always craved, "until we find an engagement ring to suit the fiancée of the Grand Duke of Karlenburgh, yes?"

"Yes!"

As if that weren't enough to keep Natalie dancing on a cloud and completely delight his sister, Sarah and the duchess, Gina and her husband arrived with the twins the next afternoon.

They were house hunting, they informed the assembled family. Jack's appointment as US Ambassador to the UN still needed to be confirmed by the Senate but the chairman of the Foreign Affairs Committee had assured him the vote was purely pro forma.

"How wonderful!" Her eyes bright with tears of joy, the duchess thumped her cane and decreed this called for a toast. "Dominic, will you and Jack pour *pálinka* for us all?"

Charlotte's heart swelled with pride as she watched her tall, gold-haired grandson-in-law and darkly handsome young relative move to the sideboard and line up an array of Bohemian cut-crystal snifters. Her gaze roamed the sitting room, lingering on her beautiful granddaughters and the just-crawling twins tended by a radiant Natalie and a laughing, if somewhat tired-looking, Zia. When Maria joined them with a tray of cheese and olives, the only one missing was Dev.

"I've been thinking," Jack said quietly as he and Dom stood shoulder to shoulder, filling delicate crystal aperitif glasses with the potent apricot brandy. "Now that your face has been splashed across half the front pages of Europe, your days as an undercover operative must be numbered."

Dom's mouth twisted. "My boss agrees. He's been trying to convince me to take over management of the organized-crimes division at Interpol Headquarters."

"A desk job in Lyon couldn't be all that bad, but why not put all this hoopla about your title and involvement in the recovery of millions of dollars in stolen art to good use?" Jack's blue eyes held his. "*My* soon-to-be boss at the UN thinks the Grand Duke of Karlenburgh would make a helluva cultural attaché. He and his lovely wife would be accepted everywhere, have access to top-level social circles—and information."

Dom's pulse kicked. He'd already decided to take the promotion and settle in Lyon. He couldn't subject Natalie to the uncertainties and dangers associated with his current occupation. But deep inside he'd been dreading the monotony of a nine-to-five job.

"Cultural attaché?" he murmured. "What exactly would that involve?"

"Whatever you wanted it to. And you'd be based here in New York, surrounded by family. Which may not always be such a good thing," Jack added drily when one of his daughters grabbed a fistful of her sister's hair and gleefully yanked.

"No," Dom countered, watching Natalie scoop the howling twin into her arms to nuzzle and kiss and coo her back to smiles. "Family is a very good thing. Especially for someone who's never had one. Tell your soon-to-be boss that the Grand Duke of Karlenburgh would be honored to accept the position of cultural attaché."

Yesterday was one of the most memorable days in my long and incredibly rich life. They were all here, my ever-increasing family. Sarah and Dev. Gina and Jack and the twins. Dominic and Natalie. Zia, Maria, even Jerome, our vigilant doorman who insisted on escorting the Brink's couriers up to my apartment. I'm not ashamed to admit I cried when they uncrated the painting.

The Canaletto my husband gave me so long ago now hangs on my bedroom wall. It's the last thing I see before I fall asleep, the first thing I see when I wake. And, oh, the memories that drift in on gossamer wings between darkness and dawn! Dominic wants to take me back to Hungary for a visit. As Natalie and Sarah delve deeper into our family's history, they add their voice to his. I've said I'll return if Dom will agree to let me formally invest him with the title of Grand Duke at the black-tie affair Gina is so eager to arrange.

Then we'll settle in until Zia finishes her residency. She works herself to the bone, poor darling. If Maria and I didn't force her to eat and snatch at least a few hours' rest, she'd drop where she stands. Something more than determination to complete the residency drives her. Something she won't speak about, even to me. I tell myself to be patient. To wait until she's ready to share the secret she hides behind her seductive smile and stunning beauty. Whatever it is, she knows I'll stand with her. We are, after all, St. Sebastians.

From the diary of Charlotte
Grand Duchess of Karlenburgh

* * * * *

Don't miss Lady Sarah's story,

A BUSINESS ENGAGEMENT

and

Lady Eugenia's story,

THE DIPLOMAT'S PREGNANT BRIDE

Available now from
USA TODAY *bestselling author Merline Lovelace*
and Harlequin Desire!

#2347 THE COWBOY'S WAY
Billionaires and Babies • by Kathie DeNosky
When a flood forces rancher T.J. Malloy to get to know his ornery neighbor Cassidy Wilson, he discovers there's something about the single mom that could spark the passion of a lifetime.

#2348 BECAUSE OF THE BABY...
Texas Cattleman's Club: After the Storm • by Cat Schield
When Lark Taylor and Keaton Holt set aside a family feud and move in together to care for their newborn niece, proximity leads to passion. But the couple's newly built bond will soon be strongly tested...

#2349 SNOWED IN WITH HER EX
Brides and Belles • by Andrea Laurence
When ex-lovers are trapped together by a blizzard, they must face the past and their long-buried feelings for one another. But can the renewed relationship survive once the snow melts?

#2350 ONE HOT DESERT NIGHT • by Kristi Gold
Sheikh Rayad Rostam and journalist Sunny McAdams have tragedy in common in their past—and undeniable chemistry in the here and now. But can they overcome their dark secrets to forge a future together?

#2351 COWGIRLS DON'T CRY
Red Dirt Royalty • by Silver James
Cowgirls don't cry—they get even...and Cassidy Morgan is about to show local mogul Chance Baron what she's made of. Too bad they just might lose their hearts in the process.

#2352 CARRYING THE LOST HEIR'S CHILD
The Barrington Trilogy • by Jules Bennett
Nash James is a billionaire—not the stable hand he's pretending to be. And when starlet Lily Beaumont reveals a pregnancy surprise of her own, he knows *all* the truths he's tried to hide will soon come to light.

REQUEST YOUR FREE BOOKS!
2 FREE NOVELS PLUS 2 FREE GIFTS!

HARLEQUIN®
Desire

ALWAYS POWERFUL, PASSIONATE AND PROVOCATIVE

HARLEQUIN®

Desire

ALWAYS POWERFUL, PASSIONATE AND PROVOCATIVE.

COWGIRLS DON'T CRY
by **Silver James**

Available January 2015

The wealthiest of enemies may seduce the ranch right out from under her!

Cassidy Morgan wasn't raised a crybaby. So when her father dies and leaves the family ranch vulnerable to takeover by an Okie gazillionaire with a grudge, she doesn't shed a tear—she fights back.

But Chance Barron, the son of said gazillionaire, is a too-sexy adversary. In fact, it isn't until Cassidy falls head over heels for the sexy cowboy-hat-wearing businessman that she even finds out he's the enemy. Now she needs a plucky plan to save her birthright. But Chance has another trick up his sleeve, putting family loyalties—and passion—to the ultimate test.

Available wherever Harlequin® Desire books and ebooks are sold.